ARLO FINCH

IN THE VALLEY OF FIRE

ARLO FINCH
IN THE VALLEY OF FIRE

JOHN AUGUST

ROARING BROOK PRESS
New York

Published by Roaring Brook Press
Roaring Brook Press is a division of Holtzbrinck Publishing Holdings Limited Partnership
175 Fifth Avenue, New York, NY 10010

mackids.com

Library of Congress Control Number: 2017944496

ISBN: 978-1-62672-814-1

Our books may be purchased in bulk for promotional, educational, or business use. Please contact your
local bookseller or the Macmillan Corporate and Premium Sales Department at (800) 221-7945 ext.
5442 or by e-mail at MacmillanSpecialMarkets@macmillan.com.

First edition, 2018
Printed in the United States of America by LSC Communications, Harrisonburg, Virginia

1 3 5 7 9 10 8 6 4 2

About the Type

The text is set in **Garamond**, a typeface based on the designs of sixteenth-century French designer Claude Garamond. It has become one of the most popular choices for print, used in everything from novels to textbooks to Field Books. Its crisp lines and even weight make it ideal for reading under the covers by flashlight.

The cover and chapter headings are set in **Cheddar Gothic**. Hand drawn by designer Adam Ladd in 2016, the typeface consists of only uppercase characters—but all twenty-six letters offer variants with extra flourishes. Cheddar Gothic was chosen for its distinctive look and adventurous spirit.

Wisdom begins in wonder.

—SOCRATES, probably

— 1 —

PINE MOUNTAIN

IT DIDN'T LOOK LIKE A HOUSE AT ALL.

True, it had many of the things you expect to see in a house—shingles, windows, bricks—but they didn't seem to be arranged in a house-like way. Instead, the building slumped against the wooded hillside like a pile of debris left over from proper homes.

To the left, a door hung six feet off the ground, no stairs beneath it. On the second floor, a blue plastic tarp stirred in the fall breeze, revealing the wooden skeleton of an abandoned room. The front door was hidden in the shadows of a sagging porch.

From the back seat of his mother's car, Arlo Finch took silent note of all the dangers he saw.

His sister, Jaycee, just said it: "It looks like a murder house."

Their mother switched off the ignition and unfastened her seat belt. Arlo knew she was counting to three. Mom counted to three a lot these days. "We should be grateful it's a house."

"I'm not sure it is," said Arlo.

They'd been driving for six hours—and three days before that—so at the very least it felt good to get out and stretch. The bright sun and cool breeze were refreshing, like jumping in a pool without getting wet.

The smell in the air reminded Arlo of the year in Philadelphia when they got a real Christmas tree from the empty lot by the gas station. Here, high in the Colorado mountains, everywhere he looked were Christmas trees, only much, much bigger. They swayed against the pale blue sky.

Their mother unlocked the U-Haul trailer behind the car.

"I need to pee," announced Jaycee.

"Me too," said Arlo.

"Well, go inside," said their mother. "Your uncle is expecting us."

Arlo followed his sister to the creaking front porch, past a rusted metal fence and stacks of lichen-covered rocks.

Jaycee was fifteen and sturdy, built like the women you

see throwing shot put in the Olympics. Back in Philadelphia and Chicago, she'd spent most days in her room watching videos on her computer and dyeing her hair different colors, emerging only for meals with an exaggerated sigh.

Arlo Finch had just turned twelve, but he looked younger. He was small, with dark hair that never stayed put. His left eye was brown, but his right eye was emerald green. *Hetero-chromia iridum* was the medical term, which made it sound like a magic spell or a disease, but it wasn't either one. *It's just how things are,* his mother said. *Like how some people have green eyes and others have brown. You have one of each.* Some teachers assumed his mismatched eyes were the reason Arlo had a hard time reading, but doctors said his vision was just fine. It was Arlo's brain that sometimes had trouble with words.

Still, he could read the sign by the front door:

SOLICITORS WILL BE SHOT AND STUFFED!

Jaycee knocked. The door slowly swung open. It hadn't been locked.

"Uncle Wade?" she called softly.

No answer. "Hello?" said Arlo, not any louder.

The house beyond the door was messy but not murder-y. Peering in from the porch, they could see stairs leading up to the second story, each step cluttered with books and boxes and bits of scrap metal. To the left, the living room had three sagging sofas and an upside-down rocking chair. To the right, a dining room table was filled with fifteen stuffed animals. Not the cuddly type you give a child, but the kind that used to be actual living creatures, like you see on field trips to the natural history museum. Arlo spotted eagles and foxes and raccoons, all frozen mid-action.

On second thought, the house was a little murder-y. But Jaycee stepped right in.

"It's trespassing!" warned Arlo in a whisper.

"Mom owns the house," she said, crossing the dining room and pushing through a swinging door.

Arlo supposed that Jaycee was technically right. According to their mother, the house had been specifically left to her when their grandparents died. But Uncle Wade lived here and always had. It was his sign by the door, and his dead animals on the table. It seemed like a bad time to argue the details of inheritance.

Still, Arlo had to pee. He followed Jaycee through the swinging door.

The kitchen was dark and cluttered, with five open cereal boxes lined up on the counter. A dead plant hung over the sink, where dishes were stacked in a few inches of greasy water.

The bathroom was down one step from the kitchen, off a hallway that looked like it had once been outside. Arlo stood at the bathroom door, shifting his weight from foot to foot, eager to get his turn after Jaycee.

Then he heard the creaks.

Heavy footsteps made their way down the wooden stairs. As if suddenly blessed with X-ray vision, Arlo could imagine exactly where the feet were landing. The sound changed as the thudding steps slowly crossed the dining room floor. And then, just as Arlo expected, the door from the dining room swung open.

But Arlo couldn't have anticipated what he saw.

The man behind the footsteps didn't look like a man, but rather a bear that had most of his fur worn off. He wore thick glasses, sweatpants and a giant T-shirt with a stain the shape of Wisconsin. (Arlo was good at geography.)

Although he'd never met him, Arlo was sure this was his uncle Wade. In the photos in his mother's album, young Wade had the same tangled red-blond hair.

The way his uncle was squinting, Arlo wasn't sure he'd been seen. But then the bear-man grumbled, "Morning."

"It's three in the afternoon." Arlo meant it to be helpful, but worried that it sounded bratty.

Uncle Wade pointed at the bathroom door. "Who's in there? Celeste?"

Celeste was their mother. Arlo shook his head. "Jaycee."

"You're Arlo."

Arlo nodded. He could hear the toilet flush. Water was running in the sink.

"You get along with your sister?" asked his uncle.

"Most times."

"You're lucky. My sister drives me crazy. Always has."

Uncle Wade only had one sister, so he was talking about Arlo's mom. This didn't seem to be a promising start.

The bathroom door opened. Wade shooed Jaycee out and shut the door behind him. Arlo was going to have to wait a little longer to pee.

———•◦•◦•———

The house only had the one bathroom, but there were plenty of bedrooms upstairs. Jaycee claimed a room at the back of the house. It was dark and smelled wet, but the door had a lock that worked.

Arlo took the room at the front of the house that had been his mom's childhood bedroom. The flowered wallpaper had faded so much that it looked like dusty snowflakes. The bedsprings squeaked, but the mattress was much softer than the one Arlo had in Chicago, or the foldaway in Philadelphia.

The windows looked out to the gravel driveway, the trees, and beyond that to the jagged, snowcapped mountains in the distance. But the view was not why Arlo had chosen this room.

He figured these windows would offer him the best chance of escape. If the house suddenly collapsed, or caught fire, or if a mountain lion entered through the creepy half-finished room at the end of the hall, he'd be able to get out quickly. He could simply tie a rope to the radiator to lower himself to the ground. Failing that, he could probably survive the jump with only a broken ankle.

A school psychologist once asked Arlo why he often imagined unlikely scenarios, like a tidal wave on Lake Michigan or gravity suddenly reversing. Did he really worry about these things happening? *No,* said Arlo, *because I'm prepared for them.*

He was only afraid of not being ready.

Arlo's father was the same way, always preparing for contingencies and surprises: *If you don't have a plan B, you don't have a plan.* But ever since his dad left—a race to the airport without time for goodbyes—it was the unimaginable things that kept Arlo awake at night, the vague fears of terrible dangers he would never see coming.

He didn't want to worry his mother and sister, so he worried for them. He took his job seriously.

Arlo decided he would need to learn the best knots for

tying sheets into a makeshift rope, and, if possible, obtain a whistle or air horn to signal the rest of the family of the rockslide. (He suspected that a rockslide was the most likely danger based on the number of yellow DANGER: FALLING ROCKS signs they'd passed on the road to Pine Mountain.)

The sun was beginning to set, casting long shadows across his room. The snowflake-flowers of the wallpaper caught the light strangely, glistening a bit in the pink glow of dusk.

Arlo wondered if he had adequately scouted the area directly beneath his window. What if it was covered with rusty iron spikes, or broken glass? He carefully leaned over the sill, looking straight down. He was glad he had. Fifteen feet below the window grew a spiky bush. It wasn't a cactus like the one he fell into in Carlsbad, or the yucca from Yuma, but it looked like something that would definitely hurt. He headed down to investigate.

Arlo's mother had gone to take the trailer back to the rental place. His sister was locked in her room, unpacking and listening to music. His uncle Wade was off in his workshop.

So as Arlo inspected the spiky plant beneath his window, he was alone. Until he realized he wasn't.

Fifty feet away, by the edge of the gravel driveway, a dog was watching him. Arlo assumed it was a dog, not a coyote or a wolf, though he had never seen either of the latter in person. The creature had a collar, which at least meant it belonged to somebody.

Arlo knew to be careful around strange dogs, but this one didn't seem threatening, only curious.

Keeping his hands low and visible, Arlo slowly walked towards it. The dog's head tilted. Its tail wagged. But as Arlo crossed some unseen line, the dog backed away.

"It's okay," said Arlo. "You don't have to be afraid." He knelt down and beckoned the dog closer.

The dog suddenly turned its attention to an empty spot of road, ignoring Arlo completely. It seemed to be staring at an invisible threat. It leaned back on its haunches, teeth bared.

The dog barked, but it didn't make a sound. It was like watching television with the volume turned off. The only way Arlo could recognize it as barking was the shaking in the dog's chest and the movement of its mouth.

Arlo knew there were breeds of Egyptian dogs that didn't bark, but he'd never imagined it would be quite like this.

The dog suddenly took off running after the unseen threat, leaving Arlo on his knees on the gravel driveway.

Arlo found his uncle padlocking his workshop and asked what the dog's name was.

"What dog?" asked Uncle Wade, confused.

Arlo described the dog, the silent barking, and how it ran away into the forest.

"Oh, that's Cooper. You saw him? He hasn't been around in a long time."

"Who does he belong to?" asked Arlo.

"He was ours, but that was years ago."

"Did he run away?"

"Nah, he died," said Uncle Wade. "He was pretty old, and dogs, well, they just don't live that long."

Arlo spent a long moment making sure he had heard correctly. He studied his uncle's face, looking for a trace of a smile, some hint that he was joking.

"If he's dead, then how did I see him?"

Uncle Wade clipped his keys back onto his belt. "Your mom didn't tell you any of this?" Arlo shook his head no. "Guess she wouldn't remember. Things are different in the mountains. Not bad, not good, just different. Gonna take you a while to get used to that, I suspect. But you'll come around."

Hearing tires on the gravel, Arlo and his uncle turned to see the station wagon returning, this time without the trailer attached. The headlights swept across them.

Uncle Wade continued. "For now, it's probably best you stay out of the forest. Just in case."

Arlo's mom got out of the car. "Would you help me bring in the groceries?" she called.

Arlo asked his uncle what was in the forest.

"Again, it's not bad, it's not good. It's just dangerous if you're not ready."

— 2 —
REASONABLE QUESTIONS

DINNER THAT NIGHT WAS SPAGHETTI with Arlo's favorite brand of sauce from a jar.

Even though he had to use a plastic fork because Uncle Wade only owned three metal forks, and even though the milk came in a thick glass bottle rather than a carton, Arlo was grateful that dinner at least tasted familiar.

They ate at the dining room table, with Uncle Wade's taxidermy animals watching them from the floor.

Taxidermy was a word Arlo learned that night. It meant taking a dead animal and making it look like it was still alive by stuffing it with sawdust and sewing it back together. It was what Uncle Wade did for money, but it was also his passion and his art—and the reason why Arlo and Jaycee were never to go into his workshop. There were dangerous chemicals inside, explained Uncle Wade, and sharp knives and power tools. Jaycee and Arlo both promised to stay out.

Jaycee asked for the wifi password. Uncle Wade said the house didn't have internet. They were too far out of town to run the wires, and he'd never really gotten the point of it anyway.

Arlo once saw a movie with a monster called Medusa who could turn a man to stone just by looking at him. That's the way Jaycee stared at Uncle Wade when he said there was no internet. Unlike the movie, Uncle Wade didn't turn to stone or even seem to notice. He simply helped himself to more spaghetti, oblivious to her petrifying gaze.

Frustrated, Jaycee turned to their mother.

"I'm sorry, Jaycee," she said. "That's just the way it is. Maybe you can use your phone."

"But phones don't work either! There's no signal. It's these stupid mountains."

Uncle Wade pointed to an old-style phone on the kitchen wall, the kind with the curly wire connected to the handset. "We got a phone right there that works great. Just keep it under five minutes in case someone's calling with an order."

Jaycee looked like she might cry or explode or both. Mom attempted to calm her down. "You can get a signal in town. I just tried at the grocery store, and I got three bars.

Plus I'm sure you'll have internet at school for doing research papers."

"We got encyclopedias, too," said Uncle Wade. "Good ones with the gold on the edges. The *M* is in two parts, and one of them is missing—I think the second one. So if you need to do a report on Montana, you're out of luck. But Mississippi or Missouri or Michigan, you're golden."

While Uncle Wade was speaking, Arlo raised his hand. He had an important question and didn't want it to go unaddressed. His mother nodded at him.

"Without the internet, how are we going to talk to Dad?" he asked.

Arlo and Jaycee's father was in China. He'd been there for three years, ever since the FBI had come to arrest him at his office in Philadelphia. They hadn't succeeded because he was already on a flight out of the country. The government said their father had broken the law by using computers to crack secret codes. Lots of people said what Arlo's father did wasn't a crime, but he couldn't risk coming back to the United States and being arrested.

So he was in China indefinitely, which Arlo learned was a word people used when they meant "more or less forever."

And that's how it felt: both endless and impermanent.

Arlo's family had always moved around a lot, but once his dad left, the moves became more frequent. First Philadelphia, then Chicago—a series of tiny apartments and houses shared with strangers. By his third school, he stopped trying to make new friends. He knew he would be unlikely to stay around long enough to make the effort worthwhile.

Through it all, the one constant was calling Dad. Every Sunday morning they video-chatted with their father on the computer. He would carry his laptop to the window of his little apartment in Guangzhou to show them the city lights—it was night there—and tell Arlo about all the weird food he'd eaten and ask how things were going in school. His dad taught him phrases in Chinese, including what he claimed were swear words.

Without the internet, how could they make their weekly call to China?

"We'll figure something out," said his mom.

Just then, the lights flickered before going out completely. The room was dark except for the dim moonlight streaming through the sliding glass door.

"It's just the wind," said Uncle Wade. "Power will be back on in a sec."

Arlo started silently counting. He could hear his uncle's fork twirling spaghetti on his plate. He could hear Jaycee breathing, and the squeak of his mother's chair. And under all that, he heard the wind rattling the windows.

Arlo got to fifty before he stopped. The lights weren't coming back on.

"Hold on," said Uncle Wade, pushing his chair back from the table. "I got flashlights."

Jaycee and Arlo washed the dishes by the light of a battery-powered lantern.

"Mom is losing it," said Jaycee as she rinsed off the bubbles.

"No she's not," said Arlo. Their mother couldn't be losing it, because Jaycee said she'd lost it back in Chicago, and that was eight days ago. Once you've lost something, you can't keep losing it again.

Arlo wasn't even sure what "it" was, but it had something to do with their mom throwing a chair through a window. Or at a window. He knew the incident involved a chair, a window and a preposition, and that it was bad enough that his mom needed to stop working at the insurance company. Within a few days, they had sold their furniture through online ads and rented the U-Haul trailer to carry what was left to Colorado.

"Listen, Arlo," said Jaycee, with a low voice that meant it

was important. "We're going to have to help out a lot more now. Mom's under a lot of stress, and we can't be adding to it. So if anything comes up, we're just going to have to deal with it ourselves and not bother her."

Arlo was shocked to hear his sister speaking this way, especially after her freak-out over the internet. This was the same girl who shouted at Mom at least twice a week, usually about rules and responsibilities. Why was she suddenly lecturing Arlo on cooperation?

"Mom doesn't want to be here, obviously," said Jaycee. "We would have come here years ago if this place wasn't the absolute last resort. It was this or be homeless."

"It's not that bad," said Arlo. "Dad sends as much money as he can."

"It's not enough. That's why I'm going to get a job after school."

"Doing what?"

"I don't know. At a store or something."

"But you hate people."

Jaycee wasn't offended. "We're all going to have to adjust. You can't be pestering Mom with every little thing. If kids at school are mean, just tough it out. If you start hearing voices again, just ignore them."

"I haven't heard the voices in a long time."

"Good," said Jaycee. "Because Mom can't handle anything more."

—•◦•—

Arlo was too old and mature to need tucking in, but he didn't object when his mother went upstairs with him to see how he had unpacked.

By flashlight, he showed her how he had sorted his clothes from head to toe, with shirts and hats going in the top drawer, pants in the middle, socks and underwear in the bottom drawer. Logically, underwear belonged in the middle drawer, but there was more room in the sock drawer. Besides, he often put his socks and underwear on at the same time, so it saved opening another drawer.

His mom agreed it just made sense.

"I was thinking, Arlo," she said. "The diner in town has really good pancakes, and I bet they have wifi, too. Maybe on Sundays we could go there with the computer to call your dad. It would be like he's having breakfast with us."

Arlo thought it was a great idea. More than that, it sounded like the kind of suggestion his mother used to make, combining something fun (pancakes) with something important (calling Dad).

Whatever the "it" was that his mother had lost, maybe she was getting it back.

He wanted to tell her about the dog he had seen—the one Uncle Wade said was dead—but he didn't want to say anything that might worry her. So, as he climbed into the almost-too-soft bed, he decided to ask it as a question: "Mom, did you ever have a dog?"

His mom sat on the edge of the bed. She was lit only by the glow of moonlight from the window. "When I was in college, my roommates and I had a dog. Her name was Rosie. She was a stray we'd found. She ended up being sort of our house mascot. Whenever we'd have a party, she'd be in every picture. I graduated and moved away, but she stayed at the house with the new batch of roommates. That's where she belonged."

"How about when you were a kid? Did you have a dog here?" asked Arlo.

"Sort of. He was mostly an outdoor dog. He only came in if it was a huge snowstorm. Even then he sort of hid."

"What was his name?"

"Cooper," she answered.

Arlo's heart skipped. His uncle was telling the truth. There really was a dog named Cooper. That was the dog he'd seen.

"Why do you ask?"

Arlo was not sure how to answer without saying too much. Luckily, his mom kept talking. "Were you thinking we should get a dog? Because we could, I guess. There's plenty of room. But we should probably get settled in here first, don't you think? Buy some forks and wash our clothes?"

Arlo agreed.

His mother neatened his hair. "I know it's scary being in a new town. New school. New friends. But we're kind of experts at this now, right?" Arlo smiled. "And I have a feeling this is going to be good. I know this house looks kind of rickety, but it's solid. It's safe. We're going to be fine."

She offered him the flashlight. He was happy she had; he'd been too embarrassed to ask for it. She kissed him on the forehead and made her way to the door. He lit her path. Just before she shut the door, he asked, "Is the forest safe?"

She paused for a moment. "Of course it is," she answered. "Just stay where you can see the house. Don't want you getting lost."

Blowing a kiss, she quietly shut the door.

After a few moments, Arlo slid out of bed and opened the window.

The moon was nearly full. As bright as it was, the light died at the edge of the forest. It was a wall of darkness, stirred only by the breeze.

Under the wind, he could hear strange birds calling, and an engine on a distant road.

The beam from his flashlight lit the area right beneath the window, but couldn't reach the spot where he'd seen the dog. He suddenly imagined what it looked like from the other side, what a creature watching from the forest would see: a bright light in the second-story window, slowly moving back and forth.

It might look like an invitation.

Arlo switched off the flashlight and shut his window, drawing the drapes closed. He climbed back in bed and slept all night without dreaming.

— 3 —
SCHOOL

THE TOWN OF PINE MOUNTAIN was so small you had to keep zooming and zooming in on the map in order to find it. Once you did, all you saw was a tiny dot inside a giant forest, accessible only by a two-lane mountain road that twisted back and forth like a lazy crayon scribble.

Pine Mountain wasn't even in the right place. Originally a mining supply camp in the 1850s, the town was destroyed in a flash flood and rebuilt further up the canyon, beyond the reach of the Big Stevens River. The gift shop, which doubled as the post office and ice cream parlor, was the only genuinely historic building in town. The rest were a haphazard collection of tiny stores, tin-roofed cabins and A-frame houses.

Pine Mountain had one bus stop, one traffic light and one school—all at the same intersection.

The school was a low brick building with a giant anchor out front. Arlo thought it was strange that a school way up in the mountains would have an anchor as its symbol. His mom said it was in honor of a famous admiral who had grown up in town and fought in World War II. Arlo's mother attended Pine Mountain when she was a girl, and actually met the admiral at a special ceremony when they dedicated the anchor.

Arlo tried to imagine his mother as a kid, but he just couldn't. The anchor had rust. His mother was even older than that rusty anchor.

The school went from kindergarten to eighth grade. Ninth graders like Jaycee had to ride a bus to Havlick, fifteen miles away. Arlo was happy to be at a different school than his sister, but disappointed to still be in elementary. Back in Chicago, sixth grade was middle school, in a completely separate building.

Arlo sat in the school office while his mom filled out paperwork. His feet hurt. His good sneakers were a little too small, but he didn't want to complain.

To his left, he could see into the nurse's office. That was where he first spotted Henry Wu, who was covered in bright purple goo.

Arlo would soon learn that Henry Wu was simply called

Wu, because there were three other Henrys in his grade. And it was easy to remember Wu, because of the goo.

The goo was in Wu's hair and eyes and ears and mouth. It bubbled out of his nose when he breathed.

Even stranger than the sticky purple fluid was the sound. Every time Wu moved, it set off a torrent of tinkling bells. It reminded Arlo of Christmas and wind chimes and pinball machines. Except that it was coming from Wu, or more precisely from the goo that was covering him.

Arlo tried to think of any other liquids that made noise like this. The ocean was loud when waves crashed against the rocks. Oil sizzled when you heated it in a frying pan.

But nothing jingled like bells—except bells. And this goo.

The school nurse, an older woman with dangly turquoise earrings, began spraying Wu with a squirt bottle, trying to rub off the purple gunk with coarse brown paper towels.

Arlo knew it was rude to stare, but he couldn't stop. He was fascinated.

"Close your eyes tight, honey," the nurse said before spraying Wu straight in the face. Whatever the goo was, it took aggressive scrubbing to get it off. And with every stroke, more bells were ringing.

At one point, Wu opened his eyes and spotted Arlo watching his de-purpling. The nurse followed his gaze, sighed, then pushed the office door shut for privacy.

Arlo looked up as his mom returned with the principal, a man with a beard and suspenders. "So, Arlo Finch. Let's get you into class."

——•◦•◦•◦•——

The sixth-grade teacher was Mrs. Mayes. She wore a necklace made of thick wooden beads and a dress with what looked to be one hundred buttons down the front.

Arlo was relieved he hadn't been asked to introduce himself to the class like at other schools. Instead, Mrs. Mayes just told him to pick an empty seat while she finished the math lesson. It was about multiplying fractions, which Arlo already knew how to do.

About ten minutes later, the classroom door opened and Henry Wu walked in. Most of the purple goo had been scrubbed away, but there were still traces around his ears. The kids reacted with hoots and laughter.

But not shock, Arlo noted. The kids thought it was funny rather than remarkable, which was odd.

In any of Arlo's other schools, if a kid walked in with purple on his face, the natural question would have been, "What happened?" But at Pine Mountain, all the students seemed to understand exactly what had happened. Many of them thought it was hilarious.

Mrs. Mayes scolded the class. "That's enough. Take your seat, Henry." But the murmuring continued.

Wu's desk was on the far side of the room. As he walked, he made faint jingling sounds, like the belled collars some cats wear. The kids tried to restrain their laughter, but holding it in just made it all funnier.

When he finally got to his desk, Wu sat as still as possible.

Arlo was one row behind him, close enough to hear when a dark-haired girl with freckles leaned over to Wu and whispered, "Did you seriously not read the Field Book?"

"I read it," Wu whispered back. "I just wanted to get one in a jar."

"The patch is Watching, not Collecting." The way she said the words, Arlo was pretty sure they were capitalized. "Next time just make a sketch."

"Indra!" said the teacher, annoyed.

"Sorry, Mrs. Mayes." Indra seemed accustomed to saying that.

As the class returned to fractions, Arlo's mind was racing. What had Wu tried to put in a jar? What was the purple goo? And how soon was recess?

The last answer came first. When the class spilled out for morning recess, Arlo stood off to the side, watching as several of the boys made passing gibes at Wu, calling him Jingle Smurf or Grapey. It didn't feel particularly mean-spirited— more like goofing around—and Wu seemed to shrug it off.

At one point, Wu shook his head like a dog after a bath to demonstrate how much jingle he had left in him.

Arlo was relieved that someone else was the center of attention. As the new kid, there was usually a spotlight on him. But because of the mysterious purple incident, no one paid him any—

"Why did you move here?" asked Indra, suddenly beside him. "Nobody moves to Pine Mountain. My family was the last, and that was three years ago, and only because the town needed a new doctor after the old one died."

"How did he die?" asked Arlo.

"He was collecting wild mushrooms—you have to be careful, because the poisonous ones look just like the good ones—when a mountain lion attacked him. He ran away, then fell off a cliff and into an icy river. Plus he was eighty-five. So, a combination of things." As she spoke, she pulled her thick hair back into an elastic. "So why did you move here?"

"My mom grew up here," said Arlo. "We have a house on Green Pass Road."

"You should watch out," said Merilee Myers, a tall girl with long curls. Her voice had a strange singsong lilt, as if everything she said was supposed to be poetry. "There's a madman who lives on Green Pass Road. He stuffs dead animals and sells them."

She was no doubt talking about Uncle Wade. Arlo just said, "Okay."

As Wu joined them, Indra pointed to Arlo. "We warned him about wild mushrooms."

"And the madman on Green Pass Road," said Merilee.

"He's got this workshop in back," said Wu. "One time, Russell Stokes snuck up to look inside, and he saw him stuffing a golden jackalope."

"What's a jackalope?" asked Arlo.

Indra, Wu and Merilee looked at him strangely, as if he'd just asked, "What's a mailbox?" or "How does a toothbrush work?" Arlo was embarrassed. In moving from school to school, had he missed some important subject? Did every kid know what a jackalope was except Arlo Finch?

"It's a rabbit with antlers," said Wu.

Arlo could picture it, mostly. But he had a harder time imagining how such a creature would hop around with antlers on its head. How would it fit into its burrow, if it had a burrow? Did rabbits even have burrows? Arlo realized he didn't know much about normal rabbits, much less rabbits with antlers.

"It's super bad luck to kill a golden jackalope," explained Wu. "Like breaking a thousand mirrors."

"Or walking under a hundred ladders," said Indra.

"Or playing with matches," said Merilee.

Arlo wondered if that last one wasn't more a bad idea than bad luck. Regardless—"He doesn't kill them," he explained. "He doesn't kill any animals. He just finds ones that are already dead and makes them look like they're alive."

Indra's eyes narrowed. "How do you know?"

"I read a book about it," said Arlo. (This was a lie.) "It's called taxidermy." (This part was true.) Arlo's answer seemed to satisfy them, but he thought it smart to change the topic completely. He pointed to the remaining purple goo under Wu's ear. "Are you going to be okay?"

"I'll take a shower when I get home," said Wu.

"Normal soap is useless," said Indra. "You'll need to use rainwater, or better yet, deer urine. Page ninety-six of the Field Book has a whole paragraph about faerie beetles."

Arlo stopped himself from asking what faerie beetles were. But then Wu turned to him. "Do they have those where you're from?"

"Of course they do," said Indra before Arlo could answer. "Faerie beetles come from the Long Woods, and the Long Woods go everywhere."

"Not space," said Wu.

"Obviously not space. But everywhere else."

With every answer he got, Arlo Finch had three more questions. What was this Field Book? What were the Long Woods? Where does one get deer urine?

But then the bell rang, and recess was over. He would have to wait until lunch.

———•◦•———

That morning, Arlo had packed a turkey sandwich, an apple and a box of juice—the same sack lunch he'd eaten every day at school in Chicago. But by the time he sat down at the long cafeteria table, he was starving. He finished his entire sandwich before even stabbing the straw into his drink.

Looking right and left, he noticed how much more food his classmates were eating. Their lunch bags were easily twice the size of his. Many kids had two sandwiches. Others had giant plastic bowls with noodles or rice. Merilee had a whole head of lettuce and a bottle of salad dressing to pour on it.

There was very little talking or horsing around. All he heard were the sounds of chewing and unwrapping.

"Aren't you hungry?" asked Wu, ripping into a whole rotisserie chicken from the supermarket.

"Yes," admitted Arlo. "Why am I so hungry?"

"It's the altitude," said Indra, spreading yellow paste on dark brown bread with seeds in it. "We're two miles up, so your body uses more calories. It's like you're a campfire, and you need to keep adding wood to keep it burning."

She offered him a chunk of her weird bread, but Arlo passed.

Gesturing with a greasy drumstick, Wu asked, "Were you in a patrol in Chicago?"

"You mean, like a gang? I wasn't in a gang. I was in the Recycling Club. We mostly just sorted through the blue trash cans and threw out paper with gum on it."

Indra clarified: "He means Rangers. Were you in Rangers?"

"I don't know what that is." Arlo took a bite of his apple, awaiting their disbelief at his ignorance.

Indra and Wu exchanged a look. They seemed excited by a new possibility.

"What are you doing tonight?" asked Indra.

"I don't know. Homework?" said Arlo, chewing his apple.

"She doesn't give homework on Tuesdays," said Wu. "It's Rangers night. You should come."

"You have to come," said Indra. "It's seven o'clock at the church."

Arlo wanted to ask which church, and what he should bring, and what Rangers actually did. But he didn't want to risk asking a question that made him seem stupid or scared or unworthy of their interest. So instead he just swallowed and said—

"Sure. I'll be there."

— 4 —
UNIFORM

"THEY LET GIRLS IN RANGERS NOW?" asked Uncle Wade.

Arlo shrugged.

"You said it was a girl who invited you to come, did you not? I presume she was not asking you to join the Girl Rangers, but rather the Rangers proper, which is to say the Boy Rangers, which was never called that because everyone knew the real Rangers were boys and the Girl Rangers were girls. We had no need for adjectives because the names were self-evident."

"I don't really know what Rangers are," said Arlo.

"Rangers are the best damn thing on Earth. Least they used to be. They probably still are. I'm just being stubborn."

They were standing in the dark and dusty basement,

where Uncle Wade was sorting through the keys on his ring, trying to figure out which one might open the heavy trunk at their feet.

"So I can go to the meeting?" asked Arlo.

"What does your mom say?"

"I haven't asked her yet. Jaycee said I shouldn't bother her with things that aren't urgent."

"That's good thinking. But she'll say yes," said Uncle Wade. "A boy who's not in Rangers is a boy without friends."

Wade found the key that fit the lock. It made a piercing scrape as it turned. He popped the latches, lifting the lid to reveal a terrifying demonic face.

"That's just a Halloween mask," said Uncle Wade, shoving it aside. The chest was full of random junk, from childhood toys to novelty pencils. Near the bottom of the chest, Uncle Wade found what he was looking for.

First he found the pants. They were dark brown with cargo pockets on the legs. Arlo knew from a glance that they were way too long for him.

"Yeah, you sew up the bottoms so they're not so long," said Uncle Wade, anticipating Arlo's objection. "The waist adjusts too, so when you put on a few pounds, they'll still fit."

He tossed the pants to Arlo and went back to digging through the trunk. The next item was a large piece of yellow cloth cut into a triangle. *Isosceles*, thought Arlo, remembering his math. It had a dark stain on it.

"Is that blood?" asked Arlo.

"Most definitely," said Uncle Wade. "A Ranger's gonna bleed from time to time. That's life on the mountain. The neckerchief's always handy for a bandage, a sling, a tourniquet. Though you'll learn you shouldn't use a tourniquet except if you're bit by a gravel snake and it's that or turn to stone."

From the term *neckerchief*, Arlo assumed the yellow triangle was worn around the neck. He didn't know what a tourniquet was, but he pledged to avoid whatever a gravel snake was and thus never be bitten by one.

The final item in the trunk was by far the most important. It was a button-down shirt covered in embroidered patches, each illustrating different symbols. The patches had been sewn on individually, and with great care. Down each arm of the shirt, small five-sided patches formed lines. Larger patches covered each pocket. Even the pocket flaps had their own patches.

The shirt itself was very dark green—darker than the darkest green crayon in the box—and reminded Arlo of the uniforms he had seen soldiers wear at parades. It smelled musty from being in the trunk, but Arlo was surprised by how strong the fabric felt. He would never have guessed it was thirty years old.

"You'll have to take the patches off," said Uncle Wade. "At least until you earn them yourself."

<hr />

Arlo sat at the dining room table, carefully snipping the threads that held the patches on the uniform.

He started with the smaller patches on the arms. Each was slightly larger than a quarter and shaped like a pentagon. At the center of each patch was a different symbol. Arlo guessed the one with a fat red cross was probably First Aid or something like it. Another patch depicted a tent, so that might be Camping.

But there were also patches with snakes and spiders and lightning bolts, and a larger one on the shirt pocket with an owl. He wanted to ask Uncle Wade what each patch stood for, but his uncle had already disappeared back into his workshop.

Arlo set the patches aside for later.

The shirt's right pocket was home to a large circular patch for "Camp Redfeather." It was more elaborate than the small patches, combining a dozen colors of thread to depict a towering purple mountain, a green forest and a deep blue lake. In the lake, Arlo could make out tiny canoes—but also a long appendage rising out of the water. He wasn't sure if it was a tentacle or a neck, but whatever creature it belonged to looked big enough to smash up the canoes and eat the paddlers.

With all the patches off, he tried on the shirt. He had expected it to be too big, but it fit perfectly.

Next came the pants. They were at least four inches too long. Arlo cuffed them as best he could, but just walking around the dining room they unrolled and dragged on the floor.

Uncle Wade had said they needed to be sewn. Arlo was sure he didn't know how to do that. Taking off patches was one thing; it was unsewing. Actual sewing was a different thing altogether.

Then Arlo had a flash of inspiration. He climbed the stairs, careful not to trip on the too-long pants.

Last winter in Chicago, Arlo's sister had started wearing safety pins on her jacket. Not just one or two, but dozens, hundreds maybe, carefully arranged in stripes and boxes. She'd spent hours perfecting the patterns, adding new pins from a cardboard box she kept on her nightstand.

Arlo was never sure if Jaycee was following a trend or attempting to start her own—he never really saw his sister's friends—but for several weeks she was obsessed with safety pins and that jacket. She was clearly proud of it.

Until one day the coat was gone.

Jaycee told her mom she had left it on the bus. Since there were still two months of winter left, they bought a wool coat from Goodwill to replace it. This time, Jaycee left it unadorned and unpinned.

But the safety pins were probably still somewhere, Arlo thought. He could picture the box they came in. So he quickly searched her room before she got home from school.

It was late afternoon. The room was already fairly dark. He switched on the desk lamp, aiming it at the dresser, which he sorted through drawer by drawer. No luck.

He tried the closet next.

Jaycee had not even started unpacking. The moving boxes were still taped up. *Maybe she doesn't think we're going to stay,* Arlo thought. *So why bother unpacking?*

If Arlo cut open the boxes, Jaycee would know he had been in her room. But how else was he going to find the safety pins?

He decided to flip the boxes over and cut through the tape on the bottom. That way, Jaycee would be unlikely to notice his work. He opened the seam just enough so he could peek inside.

That's when he saw it: the jacket.

It was the coat his sister had worn last winter, the one she claimed to have lost on the bus. Why was it here at the bottom of the box? Why had she stopped wearing it? Why had she kept it?

And why had she lied about it?

Arlo decided he didn't understand his sister at all.

Regardless, he no longer needed to find the box of safety pins. He could simply take a few from the jacket. Jaycee would never notice.

Back in his room, Arlo sat on his bed, pinning the cuffs of his Ranger pants. The fabric was heavy—thicker than denim jeans—which made it tough to wiggle the pins through. His thumbs had deep indentations from the effort.

He could hear a car's tires on the gravel driveway. Headlights swept across his room. After a few moments, two car doors opened and shut. His mom must have picked Jaycee up from the bus.

The final pin was proving very stubborn. He wiggled it and pushed with all his might. It suddenly poked through—

—right into his thumb.

Arlo gasped, more from surprise than pain. He stared at his thumbprint and the tiny hole in the center of it. A pearl of deep red blood swelled out of it.

That's when things got strange.

Arlo was still sitting on his bed, but he wasn't in his room anymore. Or at least, he wasn't just in his room. He was somewhere else at the same time, watching himself. It was like when he chatted with his dad on the computer, watching himself in the little rectangle in the corner.

Arlo could see the drop of blood on his thumb, but he could also see a boy sitting on his bed in his underwear looking at his thumb. And he sensed he wasn't alone. Someone was watching him.

He looked at the window. In the reflection, where he should have seen himself, he saw a girl instead. He guessed she was about his age, with blond hair that fell behind her shoulder. She was holding a silver hairbrush in her hand, staring directly at him. *She's looking in a mirror,* Arlo realized. *She was brushing her hair, and suddenly she saw me.*

She seemed as confused as he was.

"Who are you?" she asked. He wasn't sure she was even talking. The words may have been in his head.

"Arlo Finch," he answered. Or maybe he just thought it. Regardless, she seemed to understand.

"Are you in the Woods?"

"I'm in Pine Mountain," he said. "Do you know where that is?"

A spark of recognition, and disbelief. She knew that name.

As Arlo looked around, the walls of his room began to

vanish, revealing a moonlit forest. Only his bed remained, and the frame of the window, through which he saw the girl. The world on her side of the glass was sparkling with silver and red and gold, like a palace made of autumn leaves.

She looked off to her right. Someone was coming. Her words came in an urgent whisper: "If I can see you, they can see you. You're in danger. Be careful, Arlo Finch."

"Who is 'they'?" he asked. "Who are you?"

The girl suddenly stood up, turning her back to the reflection. She was talking with someone unseen. And then—

"Arlo!"

With a jolt, he was back in his bedroom. The girl vanished as a new shape stood in the doorway behind Arlo, blocking the light.

It was Jaycee.

"Were you in my room?" she asked.

Arlo sat in a daze. It was like waking from a dream—only he wasn't sure he was really awake. The walls had returned, but Arlo himself felt stuck between two worlds.

"Were you in my room?" she repeated, louder.

"No," he lied.

He was sure she didn't believe him, but her expression shifted. "Is something wrong?"

They stared at each other for five seconds. Arlo nearly told her about Cooper the ghost dog and the Long Woods and the girl he had been talking to in the reflection. He nearly told her that they had moved to a strange place with magical beetles and jackalopes and ominous portents. He nearly told Jaycee everything.

But then he remembered Jaycee's warning about not upsetting their mom. How precarious their situation was. How he'd promised he wasn't hearing voices anymore. So instead he said—

"Everything's fine."

They both knew it wasn't true, but they silently agreed to leave it at that. "Stay out of my room," she warned as she left.

Arlo looked down at his thumb. The blood was already dry.

5
THE MEETING

ARLO FOUND HIS MOTHER IN THE KITCHEN, trying to get the stove lit. She looked over, clearly noticing the uniform, so Arlo figured he might as well just ask: "Can I join Rangers? The meeting is tonight."

"It's fine," she said.

"Really?" he asked.

"Really. Do you want me to shorten your pants?"

"You know how to do that?" he asked. It was as if his mother had just revealed she was a part-time nuclear physicist.

"I used to sew all the time when I was your age. I was pretty good. I made my own dresses." The third burner on the stove finally lit.

"Why did you stop?"

His mother filled a pot at the sink. "I don't know. It wasn't like I decided to stop sewing. It was just something I did all the time until I didn't. That's sort of growing up, I guess. Forgetting the things you used to love."

———•◦•———

The First Church of Pine Mountain was also the Only Church of Pine Mountain. The building consisted of two tall triangles covered in wood shingles connected by a low brick rectangle.

As they pulled into the parking lot, Arlo's mother asked if he wanted her to come in with him.

Arlo unbuckled his seat belt. "I'll be fine." But he hesitated with his hand on the door latch. He was suddenly aware of his breathing.

"If they need me to sign any forms, you can just bring them home."

Arlo hadn't considered that there might be forms. What if it cost money to join? They didn't have any extra money. And what if Uncle Wade's uniform was wrong, or outdated, and they needed to buy a new uniform? What if there was a test you had to pass to even join Rangers? Arlo was consistently terrible at tests. Once, in second grade, he misspelled his own name on a spelling test. What if . . .

"Arlo?" his mom asked.

"Yes?"

"It's okay to be scared, even if there's nothing to be scared of."

"I know." His parents used to say that a lot, often after nightmares sent him running to their bed. But then she said something altogether new:

"I'll tell you, as someone with a lot more years under her belt, most of the things in life I regret are the things I didn't do. The chances I didn't take. It's easy to think of reasons to say no. It's so much better to think of reasons for yes."

Arlo looked to the church doors, where he saw kids entering the building. It was too dark and too far to see exactly who they were, or if he recognized any of them from school.

So instead he pictured himself among them, walking through those doors. He imagined a braver Arlo Finch who never worried about all the things that could go wrong and just plunged forward into the unknown. This imaginary Arlo Finch didn't ask permission in the hopes of being told no. He was more grown-up, more confident, more self-sufficient.

And he was waiting just beyond those doors.

Before he could second-guess himself, Arlo got out of the car. He walked the unlit path up to the church and pulled open the doors. The lobby was empty, but he could hear kids' voices rising from the stairwell to the right. As he walked down the steps, he felt himself becoming that other Arlo he imagined.

But first, he had a lot to learn.

Pine Mountain Company consisted of twenty-seven Rangers divided into four patrols. Arlo was assigned to Blue Patrol with Wu and Indra, apparently at their request, and immediately decided it was the best patrol in the company and possibly the entire world.

Blue Patrol was the smallest, with just six Rangers including Arlo. They were all sixth graders, except for their patrol leader, Connor Cunningham, who was in eighth but didn't act like he was their babysitter or better than them. He shook hands with Arlo, looking him in the eye. (Arlo realized later he had never shaken hands with anyone who wasn't a grownup.)

The final two members were Jonas and Julie, twin brother and sister who were homeschooled by their parents. Julie almost never spoke, but Jonas more than made up for it, offering his opinion on every small injustice he witnessed. "All the other patrols get three tents. It's unfair we only get two just because we're the smallest. Even if we don't need the third tent, we should still have it."

His rant came while the patrol was busy waterproofing the seams of their tents. Connor invited Arlo to grab a squeeze bottle and join in. As he worked, Arlo surveyed the room. Each patrol had its own corner and its own personality.

Green and Red Patrols looked to be primarily seventh and eighth graders. Red Patrol was all boys, mostly jocks, the kind who hit each other for no reason. "Last summer, one of them brought beer on a campout and they were all put on suspension for six weeks," said Wu. "They missed out on Sand Dunes, which is one of the best trips."

Green Patrol—the only one with as many girls as boys—was sitting in a circle, passing around maps. Their patrol leader, a girl with feathers woven into her hair, wrote their suggestions on a chalkboard. "That's Diana Velasquez," said Indra. "She's in tenth grade, but only because she skipped a year."

Arlo hadn't realized that some Rangers were in high school. That meant Jaycee could technically be a Ranger. He shuddered at the thought.

The fourth corner of the room was reserved for Senior Patrol, consisting of older kids who had moved up from the other patrols. Arlo guessed they were all in high school. Wu pointed one of them out. "That's Christian, Connor's brother. He's the marshal." Indeed, Christian looked almost exactly like Connor but with an extra four inches of height and twenty pounds of muscle. "The marshal is the leader of the entire company. It's a lot of responsibility."

It was only then that Arlo noticed the absence of adults. He asked Indra who was in charge.

"The Rangers run the company," explained Indra. "There are grownups—they're called Wardens—but mostly they just drive us on campouts and make sure no one cuts off a finger. Which almost never happens."

"Except for Leo McCubbin," said Wu.

"I said almost never."

Arlo wanted to ask more about Leo McCubbin and his missing finger, but just then Christian blew a whistle three times. Everyone stopped what they were doing, slowly forming a large circle at the center of the room. Arlo followed Wu and Indra's lead.

"We have a new Ranger tonight," said Christian. "Arlo Finch, please step forward to receive your colors."

Arlo heard the words, but his feet didn't comply. Wu and Indra nudged him until he finally moved.

"Arlo Flinch," whispered a freckled Red Ranger, proud of himself. Christian glared at him, shutting him up.

"Blue Patrol Leader, do you take this Ranger under your watch?" asked Christian.

"I do," said Connor.

"Then present his colors. Rangers, salute."

All of the Rangers put their right fists to their chests. Arlo followed their lead.

"Repeat after me," said Christian. Arlo nodded.

Loyal, brave, kind and true—
Keeper of the Old and New—

Connor stood in front of Arlo, unfolding a new blue neckerchief, the same color as the rest of his patrol's. Arlo felt stupid for not realizing the patrol colors matched the neckerchiefs. He hadn't worn Uncle Wade's, mostly because of the bloodstain, but also because he wasn't sure how to tie it. It was still bunched up in his pocket.

Placing the blue neckerchief around Arlo's collar, Connor slid a metal ring up to fasten it.

I guard the wild,
Defend the weak,
Mark the path,
And virtue seek.

Forest spirits hear me now
As I speak my Ranger's Vow.

With the oath finished, everyone relaxed out of their salutes. Arlo put his hand down. His palm was sweaty.

Christian made it official. "Arlo Finch has taken his Ranger's Vow. May his path be safe."

All the other Rangers spoke in unison: "May his aim be true."

— 6 —
THE FIELD BOOK

THE RANGER FIELD BOOK WAS PAPERBACK, an inch thick, and heavy. The pages were crisp and smelled new, but the text and illustrations seemed old, like it hadn't been updated in decades.

Arlo received his Field Book after the meeting. The company quartermaster, a girl in Senior Patrol, took one from the locked cabinet in the supply room. With a black marker, she wrote *FINCH* on the top edge of the book in big letters. "You're only issued one," she said. "So don't lose it."

Arlo couldn't imagine ever letting it out of his sight. It was too dark to read on the car ride home, but the illustrations were mysterious and fascinating: traps and creatures and canoeing techniques. The back of the book showed the various patches. He spotted some of the ones from Uncle Wade's shirt, but many more as well, featuring animal tracks, flaming arrows and watchtowers.

He wanted to stay up all night reading the book—yet at the same time, he wanted to save it so he could read it page by page. As he flipped past a drawing of tents, he suddenly remembered: "There's a campout this weekend. I can go, right?"

"Of course," his mom said.

As they pulled into the driveway, Arlo spotted Cooper standing watch in the moonlight. He wondered if there was anything in the Field Book about ghost dogs.

There just had to be.

That night in bed, Arlo studied the book by flashlight until his batteries ran out.

The Field Book covered constellations, topographic maps, flag-folding, fire-building, boot maintenance, snakebites, avalanches, water purification, knots, ticks, totem lore, bears, poisonous plants, snare traps, hiking, tracking, knife-sharpening, first aid, shock, packing, stick biscuits, smoke signals, trail signs, lashing, woodlore, edible plants, slings, splints, compound fractures, stretchers, conservation and tornadoes.

It had nothing to say about ghost dogs, however.

In fact, the only reference for *ghost* in the index was a page warning about the dangers of camping in graveyards. The listing for *spirit* featured thirty-four entries, but most of them were for spirit in the sense of "teamwork" rather than "disembodied supernatural entity."

The back third of the Field Book was devoted to ranks and badges. Arlo couldn't make sense of it by flashlight, but Indra and Wu filled in the details the next day at school.

There were five ranks in Rangers: Squirrel, Owl, Wolf, Ram and Bear.

Even without looking at the patch on the left shirt pocket, it was pretty easy to guess a Ranger's rank. The youngest ones were Squirrels. Most eighth and ninth graders were Owls. The older ones were Wolves and Rams.

And no one was a Bear, because there were no Bears.

Wu, Indra and the twins were all Squirrels. Their rank patches depicted a bushy-tailed squirrel in profile, an acorn held in its front paws. Being the youngest members, Squirrels took a fair amount of teasing, gentle and otherwise. Wu recounted how, during a recent campout, Red Patrol had yelled, "Feed the squirrels!" while raining pinecones down on Blue.

Connor was an Owl, as were most of the patrol leaders. His rank patch showed a hunting owl in flight, its wide wings curving up while its talons bore down. Earning Owl required seven specific skill patches, many of which Indra had already earned. (Wu had been gooed by a faerie beetle while trying to finish his Watching.)

Senior Patrol was almost entirely Wolves. Their rank patches featured a howling wolf, its head tipped up to the sky. It took most Rangers four years to earn Wolf, although Indra calculated it was possible to do it in as little as two and a half with proper planning and a valid passport. "You would need to go to Australia or New Zealand over Christmas break, which is our winter but their summer, and join a company that is headed to camp, and get elected patrol leader. While you're there you get your Leadership and Tracking patches, half a year earlier than you could have here." Indra had gone as far as researching a Ranger company in Auckland that might work, but was waiting until her next birthday to share the idea with her parents.

With massive curled horns set against a floating head, the Ram patch looked more dragon than sheep. Christian Cunningham and two other high school kids were the only Rams in the company. "Most kids never get to that rank," Wu explained. "There's a ton of stonecraeft and weathering, which are super hard. It's basically math but with rocks and clouds."

The Bear patch was the most unusual, because it didn't depict a bear at all, but rather a leafless tree. Arlo had seen it only in the Field Book, because no Ranger in Pine Mountain Company had achieved the rank for a dozen years. Christian was said to be going for his, but dodged the question when asked directly. Wu said the training, called the Vigil, required leaving Colorado for weeks at a time, with strict secrecy over exactly what was taught. "It's super Jedi ninja stuff."

As a new member, Arlo was unranked, with no patch on his pocket.

He was the only unranked Ranger in the entire company, but that was simply because of timing. At the start of every summer, five or six new kids joined Rangers, all starting from zero like Arlo. By September, they invariably earned Squirrel.

Joining in the late fall put Arlo behind, but he was determined to catch up. In order to achieve the rank of Squirrel, he would have to meet the rank requirements in the back of the Field Book:

Repeat from memory the Ranger's Vow. He was already off to a bad start. The Vow was only thirty-five words long, but they simply wouldn't stick properly in his head. By the time he got to "defend the weak," his mind had wandered away.

It was that way with most things Arlo had to memorize. After six years of daily recital at various elementary schools, he still fumbled his way through the Pledge of Allegiance. At baseball games, the national anthem was completely befuddling, the rockets' red glare seeming to have wandered in from another song altogether.

Demonstrate the Ranger's salute. This was easy. To salute, you placed your right fist over your heart, knuckles touching your chest. Your thumb needed to be flat against your curled fingers, in line with your arm, never giving the thumbs-up sign or, worse, tucked inside the fist.

Spend three nights camping with your patrol. There was a campout every month, including one this weekend.

Show how to tie the ten Ranger's knots. Explain how each is used. Arlo studied the illustrations in the Field Book. Even with the arrows, it was tough to get them right, but it felt like the kind of thing that just required practice.

Demonstrate your proficiency with the Ranger's compass. Arlo didn't have his Ranger's compass yet, but Wu had described the process for the test: "They give you a shape, like a triangle or a cross, and you have to walk that pattern, ending up at exactly the same spot you started. The hardest part is keeping your paces even." Wu completed it on his first try, but it had taken Indra three attempts.

Successfully complete your Trial of Rank. Once he had finished all the other requirements, Arlo would have to demonstrate what he'd learned in front of a panel of Rangers and answer their questions. "You don't know who is on your panel until you get there," said Wu. "And they can ask you anything, like how deep you're supposed to bury your poop or the difference between kinnikinnick and bearberry. At the end, they vote, and if you don't pass, you have to wait three months until your next trial."

"You have to be prepared for anything," said Indra.

With the Field Book in his hands, Arlo felt like he actually could be ready. From patches to pinecones, sunburns to signal fires, the book made the Ranger universe seem orderly.

That Friday afternoon, as he packed his backpack according to the book's lists and illustrations, he didn't worry that he was forgetting anything. As long as he followed the instructions, everything would be fine. When it came to Rangers, the Field Book had all the answers.

Except for the questions Arlo hadn't thought to ask.

—7—
THE WONDER

ARLO COULD NOT BELIEVE HOW FAR THEY HIKED. Every time he thought they had reached the top of the mountain, the trail just kept going, with another peak ahead.

The distance was not the problem. Arlo was used to walking. Back in Chicago, they would often walk a mile to the museum, even in the winter when it was so cold it hurt to breathe and his ears started ringing. But Chicago was flat. Everything in Colorado was on a slope. And there were always rocks to step over, or step around. Did it take more energy to step over or around a rock? He wanted to ask, but he was too tired to speak.

His only consolation was that the hike seemed to be just as exhausting for Wu and Indra. Back when they'd first put on their packs at the car, they were discussing whether hammocks counted as beds or not. Wu was convinced they did. After all, you could sleep in a hammock. Indra said that by Wu's logic, anything a person could conceivably fall asleep in was a bed, be it a couch, a car or an airplane. Wu and Indra both tried to sway Arlo to their side, but by the end of the first half mile, the argument was abandoned unresolved.

The entire company was hiking to Ram's Meadow, one of their frequent campsites. Responsibility for planning the monthly camping trip rotated among patrols. This time it was Green Patrol's turn. They had chosen Ram's Meadow after a lengthy discussion and three rounds of secret ballot. Wu said Blue Patrol always picked Three Creeks, which apparently had the best fishing. Arlo had never been fishing, and did not like fish, but was certain his patrol was correct in their choice.

"Hold up," whispered Connor. He stopped them, then pointed to something deep in the forest.

"Wow," whispered Wu, impressed.

Indra agreed. "I can't believe it's so close."

"Cool," whispered Arlo. But he didn't notice anything, no matter how hard he looked. All he could see was trees. All he could hear was his pulse in his ears. Yet his entire patrol seemed to be watching something remarkable. Arlo tried to follow their gaze. Connor must have spotted his frustration, because he waved him over closer. With just a tiny shift to the left, Arlo saw it.

It was a deer, or an elk—Arlo wasn't sure what to call this creature he had only seen in picture books—standing just off the trail, watching them. It was so close that Arlo could see the glint in its black eyes and the texture of its fur. He could watch it breathing. More than any creature he had ever encountered in the wild, Arlo felt that this one had a name, a family, a story.

And then, BOOM!

From behind them, a cannon shot. The deer took off running, terrified. Arlo looked back to see Red Patrol approaching. One of the boys wiggled his hands and clapped them together. The resulting noise was a thousand times louder than expected, a true explosion. Arlo felt his heart skip.

"Not cool, Russell," said Connor.

"It's a deer. Get over it." The boy's name was Russell Stokes. Arlo recognized him as the one who'd called him Arlo Flinch at the meeting.

Red Patrol skirted past them on the narrow trail. There were icy glares and grumbles, but no words were exchanged.

Once they were out of earshot, Arlo asked, "What was that? How did he do that?"

"It's called a thunderclap," said Wu. "You don't learn that until you reach Owl."

"But what is it?" Arlo asked as they started hiking again. "I mean it's like, well it's . . ." He racked his brain for a different term, something that would explain what he meant without seeming crazy, but ultimately only one word made sense: "It's magic."

"It's not magic," said Indra.

Wu agreed. "Magic is spells and stuff. Rangers don't do that." Off Indra's look, he quickly added, "Well, we're not supposed to do that."

"But what Russell did is impossible," said Arlo. "It's not natural. People can't do that."

The trio hung back a bit from the rest of the group so they could talk privately.

"Do you know how to walk on a tightrope?" asked Indra.

"No," said Arlo.

"But you've seen people walk on tightropes, like on TV. You know it's a thing people can do."

"Yes."

"So how do you think they do it?"

"They learn. They practice."

"Exactly. A thunderclap is a skill, just like walking on a tightrope. Just because most people can't do it doesn't mean it's magic."

"But why wouldn't I have seen it before now?" said Arlo.

"Because it only works in certain places," said Wu.

Indra held out her left hand. "Imagine this is the normal world. Every place you've ever been. Every city. Every town." She then held out her right hand. "Imagine this is the Long Woods. It's not our world, but it's right next door. Normally, you would never see it, never know it's there. Except there are some places where the two worlds brush up against each other." She slid her hands past each other, barely touching. "When they do that, it creates friction. Energy."

"Like static electricity?" asked Arlo.

Indra and Wu exchanged a look, impressed. Arlo was getting it. "These mountains, they have a lot of that energy. And if you know how to use it, how to focus and shape it, you can do things with it."

"When do I learn?" asked Arlo.

"You already started," said Wu. "You're a Ranger now."

— •◆•—

Ram's Meadow was worth the hike.

Two-thirds of the way up a mountain, the clearing had vast fields of wildflowers and massive boulders that looked like the toes of giants. Rabbitlike creatures called pikas kept watch from the lichen-covered rocks.

After some squabbling with Red Patrol over campsites, the Blues picked their spot and set up their tents. Dinner was hot dogs and beans cooked over the fire. Both were extra delicious from the smoke and exhaustion.

Arlo had never sat around a campfire before. It was strangely hypnotic, like watching a television with only one channel. Logs slowly disintegrated into glowing embers. White flakes of ash fluttered up, carried by invisible currents.

A flash of light caught his attention. Far in the distance, a few of the Senior Patrol Rangers were standing in a line. One by one, they were pointing their fingers, sending out streaking white plumes of light that arced across the night sky before slowly dimming and falling.

"Are those fireworks?" asked Arlo.

"They're snaplights," said Indra.

"It's like you're snapping your fingers," explained Connor. "But instead of sound, you make light." He stood and demonstrated. With a flick of his hand, he snapped his fingers. A bright flare of light erupted, shooting away like a tiny comet. "It's all light, no heat, so you can't catch anything on fire. Rangers use them all the time. They're better than flashlights."

Arlo tried, but nothing happened. It was like he was trying to get someone's attention and failing.

"Imagine the air is a piece of paper," said Connor. "You're trying to form a sharp crease. The light follows that edge."

"It's all about the timing," explained Wu. He demonstrated,

but the light barely left his fingertips. It fizzled out before it even really started.

Indra's snaplight was more like a firefly, a faint glow that quickly dimmed.

Twins Julie and Jonas had slightly better snaplights, each lasting about three seconds. Their older sister had been in Rangers, so they'd learned from her.

None of their snaplights could compare to Connor's. He could send three in quick succession, or bounce them like a stone skipping across a lake.

Arlo kept trying, but all he achieved was sore fingers.

"You'll get it eventually," said Connor. "It takes a couple of months."

Watching the lights zip across the meadow, Arlo reminded himself that it wasn't technically magic, but it sure felt like it. "Why doesn't anyone ever talk about this?" he asked. "Snaplights and thunderclaps—people in Chicago or Philadelphia, they'd be amazed. Why don't I see videos of it on the internet?"

"It's called the Wonder," said Connor. "You can't photograph it, or record it. You can only see it for yourself."

Wu skewered another marshmallow to roast. "It's like when there's a full moon and it looks giant. But then when you take a picture of it, it's actually normal size."

"It's nothing like that," said Indra. "You're talking about

64

an illusion. Snaplights and thunderclaps are real. They just can't be photographed."

"Like the giant moon!"

"You'd still have a photo of the moon! It just wouldn't look big. If you try to take a picture of a snaplight or a faerie beetle, it doesn't show up at all."

"But you could tell someone about them," said Arlo. "You could describe them, what they're like."

"No one would believe you," said Wu, blowing out his flaming marshmallow. "That's the Wonder. The same reason this stuff only works here, it only makes sense here."

"And places like here," added Connor. "There are Rangers all over the world."

"Because the Long Woods go everywhere?" guessed Arlo.

"Exactly," said Connor. "But the farther you get from the edge of the Long Woods, the less Wonder there is. It's not just snaplights and thunderclaps—it's the actual idea of them. It fades away like a dream."

Arlo thought about his mother growing up in Pine Mountain. She must have known about these things as a kid. But over time, those memories had disappeared.

He felt sorry for his mom. Her childhood must have been full of Wonder, but she couldn't remember it.

"Even in town, the Wonder isn't nearly as strong," said Jonas. "You can't do a snaplight or anything. Our mom doesn't even think about it. She has no idea what we can do up here."

"But adults in town know about the Long Woods, don't they?" asked Arlo. He turned to Wu. "Like the nurse at school: she was helping you clean off the purple goo. So she must know about faerie beetles."

"Not really," said Wu. "It's weird. Most adults, it's like they know but they don't know. They'll always find some other explanation."

Connor agreed. "My dad was in Rangers when he was a kid. But when you ask him about it, it's clear he doesn't really remember it right. It's like his memories are in black and white rather than color."

"One theory is that the Wonder is like a natural defense," said Indra. "It's how the Long Woods stay secret: by making you forget they even exist."

Connor was called away for a patrol leaders' meeting to discuss plans for tomorrow. Around the campfire, Wu observed how much better Connor was at snaplights and thunderclaps.

"It's not surprising, considering what he's been through," said Indra. "He'd have to be better, just to survive."

"What do you mean?" asked Arlo.

She'd clearly expected him to ask the question. "So, all

this happened when we were little. Like, three years old. So it's not like we remember it ourselves."

"But everyone knows," said Wu. "Our parents have told us about it."

"Our sister was there," added Jonas, roasting a marshmallow. "She was in kindergarten with both of them."

"Both of who?" asked Arlo.

"And Connor will talk about it sometimes," said Indra, "but you don't ever want to bring it up." Everyone looked to see that Connor was still out of earshot. "So, back when Connor was, like, five or six, his family went camping at Highcross. It's really pretty, but we never go there anymore."

"Obviously," said Wu.

Indra continued. "Connor was there, and his brother Christian, and their cousin Katie. They were playing hide-and-seek. Christian was looking for them, but he couldn't find them anywhere. He was yelling for them. No answer. It was starting to get dark, so he told his parents. No one could find Connor and Katie. That night, the whole town began looking for them. There were search parties and tracking dogs. They had helicopters flying in from Denver."

"They even had psychics and shamans and stuff," said Wu.

"How did they find them?" asked Arlo.

"They never did." Indra paused for dramatic effect. "The

search went on for three weeks, and eventually they called it off, because there was no way anyone could still be alive out there."

Arlo was confused. "But Connor is alive."

"A month after they disappeared, Connor suddenly showed up in Canada, thousands of miles away. No one could explain how he'd gotten there. Connor couldn't remember anything after he'd been playing hide-and-seek. He had no idea where Katie was."

"They never found her?" asked Arlo.

"No," said Wu. "No trace at all."

"Our mom says the trolls got her," said Julie. It was the first time she had spoken in an hour.

"There are trolls?" asked Arlo.

"In the Long Woods? Of course. The Field Book doesn't even list half the things you'd find there," said Indra. "Officially, the police say that someone must have kidnapped the two of them, and Connor got away. But everyone here knows that they probably crossed into the Long Woods somehow. That's why no one could find them, because they weren't even in our world anymore. Somehow Connor found his way out, but in Canada rather than Colorado."

"Because the Long Woods go everywhere," said Arlo.

"Exactly," said Wu. "And distances there aren't the same. You could walk ten miles through the Long Woods and end up in Brazil."

"The hardest part is not dying," said Indra. "Most grown-ups, even Wardens, they couldn't last one night in the Long Woods. For a five-year-old to survive out there for a week, much less a month, is unheard of."

His meeting over, Connor was headed back to the campfire. They needed to wrap this up. But first, Arlo had to ask an important question: "Connor's cousin—if she was still in the Long Woods, she'd be about our age now, right?"

"I guess. But there's no way she could still be alive," said Wu.

As he drank his clumpy hot chocolate, Arlo pictured the girl he'd seen in the reflection, and the way she'd reacted when he had said "Pine Mountain." The thoughts came to him in a rush.

Maybe she knew the name Pine Mountain because it was where she used to live.

Because she was Connor's missing cousin.

And if so, Arlo was the only one who knew she was alive.

— 8 —

LIGHTS IN THE DARK

ARLO WOKE UP CONFUSED ABOUT WHERE HE WAS.

In the dim light, he saw fingerlike shadows above him, swaying back and forth. To his right, an unseen animal was growling.

Worse, his arms were immobilized, pinned at his side. He started to panic.

Then he remembered he was camping.

The tent, which had seemed so spacious when they first set it up, was a lot smaller with their sleeping bags out. Jackets were piled on top of boots by the zippered door.

The growling animal was Wu. He snored in a way that seemed impossible, making noise on both the inhale and the exhale. It wasn't particularly loud, except that everything else was so quiet. Arlo could hear the wind in the grass, and the burbling of a distant stream. It was like turning up the static on a radio, hearing the background noise as music.

Arlo's arms really were pinned, but it was because the sleeping bag was so narrow. Connor called them "mummy bags," but they were more like cocoons, or puffy down parkas for your body. They tapered until there was just enough room for your feet.

Connor's bag was brand-new, top-of-the-line, designed for climbers scaling Mount Everest. It came from a catalog that sold collapsible kayaks and tiny stoves.

Arlo's sleeping bag came from the back of the quartermaster's supply closet. It had probably been used by fifty different Rangers over the years. It smelled like nylon and spit and smoke and sunscreen, but he had to admit it kept him plenty warm. The night air was cold on his cheeks, but his body was toasty.

He turned over and tried to fall back asleep.

His pillow was actually his hooded sweatshirt, folded up on itself and wrapped in its hood, just the way Wu had shown him. It was comfortable enough. But there was a rock somewhere under his hip. It took a lot of wiggling to find a position where the rock didn't poke him.

And then he realized he needed to pee.

Or did he?

Could he wait?

After all, it was going to be morning soon, he assumed, not really having any idea of the time, and not having a watch, but certain that it had to be nearer to morning than night considering he'd fallen asleep and woken up.

Arlo decided he could wait. It would be easier if he waited.

Then he heard a beep. It was a single, low digital chime. It came from behind him.

Arlo rolled over to face Wu. The slumbering growler had his arm out over his sleeping bag. And on his wrist, a digital watch.

Arlo snaked his hand out of his bag and carefully tapped Wu's watch until he found the backlight.

It was midnight. Midnight. He'd only been asleep two hours. It was another six hours until dawn. There was no way he was going to make it until morning to pee.

Arlo unzipped his bag as quietly as he could, careful not to wake Connor or Wu.

He found his boots easily enough. He didn't bother lacing them tight.

Connor's coat was on the top of the pile. The jacket had no doubt come from the same catalog as Connor's sleeping bag, designed for alpine adventures by bearded men wearing mirrored sunglasses that wrapped tight to the face like goggles. The parka had seventeen pockets and special loops for hanging accessories. It had so many different trade-marked fabrics it was probably bulletproof.

Arlo's coat was at the bottom of the pile. It only had two pockets, with snaps rather than zippers, and a drawstring hood with the cord half pulled out. The cuff of the right sleeve was still wet from where he had spilled hot chocolate earlier.

And then a thought occurred to Arlo: just wear Connor's coat.

Connor wouldn't know or care. In fact, if Connor were awake, he would probably say, "Why are you even asking? Of course you can wear it." Connor would say this because Rangers are kind—it's in the Vow. It would be kind for Connor to let Arlo wear his amazing coat rather than the crappy coat with the snap pockets and hot chocolate on the cuff.

And once this offer was made, it would likewise be kind for Arlo to say yes. *Kind* meant nearly the same thing as *polite,* and the opposite of *polite* was *rude,* and there was never a good reason to be rude.

So in the spirit of kindness, Arlo put on Connor's parka.

It was amazing, like sliding your arms into a daydream. He never wanted to take this coat off.

He unzipped the tent just enough to slip outside.

The night air was bracingly cold, and immediately snapped Arlo out of his half slumber. Still, Connor's incredible coat kept his torso warm. Even the pockets were lined with microfiber fleece.

Without the campfire's orange glow, the tents looked dark and deserted, clustered together like sleeping rhinos. Arlo realized he was probably the only Ranger awake. Even the adults were sleeping.

He was maybe the only person awake in the whole valley.

Arlo looked up, amazed to see so many tiny lights. It was a moonless night. All the spaces between the bright stars revealed smaller, dimmer stars. Just above the trees, he could make out a broad smear of light—the Milky Way, or at least an arm of it. He had seen it in the planetarium in Chicago, but never in real life.

Standing alone in the forest under ten thousand sparkling stars, Arlo Finch felt small—but not in a bad way. Rather, it felt like being let in on a secret about the vastness of the universe, a goldfish set loose in the ocean.

As his breath fogged the night air, Arlo spent a few

moments in quiet contemplation. He wondered if his father saw the same stars in China. He wondered how many of these stars had names, and who named them, and if they ever just gave out goofy names like Snarklebutt, because why not?

Arlo wondered if some kid on a planet circling one of these stars was looking in Earth's direction wondering the same things. Given how many billions of stars there were in the universe, it seemed likely—maybe inevitable—that there were other worlds almost like this one. Arlo's mind was racing.

And his bladder was full. He really had to pee.

He headed off for the trees. He wasn't sure how far from the tents was the appropriate distance to urinate. Tomorrow, he'd look it up in the Field Book. Tonight, he'd just trust his instincts.

At the edge of the clearing, he found a tree suited to the purpose. As he was finishing up, he spotted something.

A light.

It was deeper in the forest—the size of a flashlight, but definitely not a flashlight. Arlo watched as the light bobbed and weaved among the trees. It was floating, or flying.

Or dancing. There was no music, but Arlo sensed that it was moving to a rhythm, its light growing slightly brighter or dimmer to a steady beat.

Suddenly, there was another light. It was the same size, but slightly pinker. The two lights swirled, chasing each other like birds at the park. The faster they moved, the more they seemed to blur, leaving smoky, sparkling trails in the air.

Arlo moved closer, careful not to spook them.

As best he could tell, they were just glowing spheres of light. Each was the size of a baseball, with no visible wings. Which meant it was impossible for them to fly. But ghost dogs and faerie beetles were similarly impossible, and they both seemed to be real, so Arlo's skepticism was dialed pretty low these days.

Arlo wondered if these were snaplights that had somehow come alive. He had seen the older Rangers casting snaplights that hung in the air for twenty seconds before slowly falling. What if some snaplights never fell, but instead lived on?

Then he thought, *What if this is the Wonder?* All the impossible things which suddenly aren't.

A twig snapped under Arlo's foot. The dancing lights seemed to hear it, stopping their chase to hover for a moment. Arlo froze.

Could they see him? Did they even have eyes?

The lights eventually began swirling again, heading deeper into the forest. Arlo was determined to be stealthier this time, carefully moving from tree to tree so they wouldn't notice him.

The ground under his feet was becoming muddier. He regretted not tying his boots—the laces were dragging in the muck. But he couldn't stop to fix them, because the lights were moving faster. It was tough to keep them in sight while trying to stay somewhat hidden.

One of the lights flew straight up, circling a tall tree. Arlo watched as it hid among the branches, growing dim as the other light searched for it. It was sneaky, carefully keeping on the far side of the trunk. Arlo crept closer, never taking his eyes off them.

Suddenly, the second light zoomed past Arlo, so close he could feel a whoosh. These things had some substance after all.

The glowing sphere hung in front of Arlo, suspended in midair. And then it winked. Or blinked. It got dimmer for just a second, but Arlo could swear it was deliberate. *I see you*, it was saying. And it wasn't afraid.

Arlo felt he should say something. "Hello?"

The light blinked again.

"What are you? Did someone make—"

Before he could finish his question, the light suddenly flew off, joining its friend deeper in the forest. Arlo followed them. This time, he didn't worry about being stealthy. He ran to catch up with them.

The lights slowed, then stopped, apparently waiting for him to catch up. They gradually rose higher and higher. Arlo hurried to keep them in sight when suddenly—

BOOOOOOM!

A massive thunderclap rang through the forest. Arlo nearly jumped out of his skin.

A boy's voice yelled, "Stop!"

Arlo searched amid the dark trees. A snaplight suddenly flared, revealing Connor a hundred feet behind him. Connor wasn't wearing a coat, and Arlo suddenly realized why.

"I'm sorry!" yelled Arlo. "I didn't think you'd . . ."

"Don't move!" Connor sent up two more snaplights and slowly approached.

Arlo looked up to the glowing lights he had been following. They were circling each other, watching. With the illumination from Connor's snaplights, he could see there was more to them. Swirling shadows surrounded them, like bones made of smoke.

"What are they?"

"Wisps," said Connor. "They're trying to kill you."

Connor aimed another snaplight just past Arlo's feet, revealing the edge of a pit. Six feet below, sharp wooden spikes pointed up like spears. It was a simple but deadly trap, and Arlo had run right up to the edge of it.

One more step and Arlo Finch would have been skewered. He carefully backed away.

Connor moved beside him. "Cover your ears."

Arlo plugged his ears tight. Connor rubbed his hands

together in a special way and then clapped them, sending another crashing boom of thunder at the wisps.

The living lights swirled. Arlo sensed they were angry, or confused. Their plan of leading him to the trap had nearly worked.

The lights bobbed, circled, then flew off deep into the forest, out of sight.

Turning around, Arlo could see flashlights and snap-lights as other Rangers and Wardens came to investigate the thunderclaps.

Connor sent up a snaplight to show where they were.

"Are you boys all right?" yelled one of the Wardens.

Connor yelled back, "We're fine!" He then whispered to Arlo, "Don't say anything about the wisps. They'll make us go home tonight."

———•◦◉◦•———

The Wardens believed Connor's story about Arlo getting lost in the woods, but Indra didn't. As soon as the adults left, she snuck into their tent and demanded the real story.

With Connor's blessing, Arlo told her and Wu exactly what had happened.

"Why would wisps be this far out of the Long Woods?" asked Indra.

"I don't know," said Connor.

"Maybe they were hungry," suggested Wu. "It says in the Field Book that they lure creatures to their death to eat their souls."

"Then who made the trap?" asked Arlo. "They don't have hands. Someone had to build that."

"And it wasn't an old trap, either," said Connor. "We camp up here all the time. We would have seen it before."

Indra was certain she had the answer. "Someone built the trap, and sent the wisps to lure you into it. It wasn't an accident or a coincidence. It was planned."

Arlo was reeling. "You're saying that someone is trying to kill me?"

"Of course not," she said. "They were trying to kill Connor. You were just wearing his coat."

9
THE GOLD PAN

THE GOLD PAN WAS PINE MOUNTAIN'S ONLY RESTAURANT, unless you counted the hot dogs at the gas station.

The little diner had been operating in the same spot as long as anyone could remember. Framed photos on the walls showed the building with every era of car parked in front of it—even some horses. In one picture, two men with shovels were carving a path through a massive snowdrift to the door. Only the Gold Pan sign on the roof was visible.

"That was your grandfather," said Arlo's mom, pointing to one of the men.

Arlo squinted, but he couldn't see any details in the man's face. The black-and-white photo was grainy, and the glass in the frame had a layer of dust and grease.

"Did Granddad work here?" asked Jaycee as she set up the laptop in a corner booth.

"No, but the snow that year was so bad everyone had to help out. The town was cut off for weeks until they finally got the pass back open."

Jaycee's laptop made a familiar series of bloops. "We're connecting," she said. Arlo slid in next to her in the booth, watching as gibberish scrolled up the laptop's screen. Because of what happened with the FBI, they had to use special software to talk with their father in China.

"You smell like a sweaty campfire," said Jaycee. Arlo sniffed his sleeve, but he couldn't smell it. She was probably right. Arlo had come straight from the campout.

Suddenly, his father was on the screen. "Hey kiddos. How's life on the mountain?" The video stuttered a bit, but eventually sharpened. Arlo's dad was skinny and bearded, with glasses that seemed an essential part of his face. Arlo was relieved that as crazy as things seemed, his dad remained exactly the same.

Over pancakes and french fries—it was more lunchtime than breakfast—Arlo and Jaycee filled their father in on what had happened since they'd arrived in Pine Mountain. Arlo omitted a few things, like nearly being killed in a pit of sharp spikes by glowing wisps that came from the Long Woods.

And he left out other details, such as thunderclaps and snaplights and Cooper the ghost dog who kept silent watch over the house.

He mostly told his father about school ("It's fine.") and Rangers ("It's fun.").

Jaycee did the bulk of the talking anyway, describing in detail her classes and her locker and why she was thinking about switching from clarinet to drums in marching band. She said that one of the snares had come down with mononucleosis, which sounded like something from a superhero movie but was actually really common, and that left an opening for a new drummer. Arlo marveled at how different Jaycee was when she was talking with their father. In normal life, she was grouchy and sullen. But with Dad, she lit up, smiling and laughing.

Their mom didn't chime in much. Arlo knew his parents e-mailed and sometimes spoke on the phone, particularly about money and this lawyer in California who was trying to make it safe for his dad to come back to the States. The video calls were just for Arlo and Jaycee, so it wouldn't feel like their dad was so far away.

After about fifteen minutes, a familiar alert popped up in the corner of the screen. It warned they were "losing the proxy," which meant they had less than ten seconds before the call would drop. Squeezing to fit in front of the camera, they each gave a quick "love you" and "bye." Then the connection terminated.

They were left hugging themselves, watching a frozen, pixelated image of their dad. Jaycee took a screenshot and added it to a folder.

While Arlo finished his pancakes, his mom went to the counter to pay the bill.

Jaycee kept her voice low, which was never a good sign. "I'm getting a job."

"Where?" asked Arlo.

"Here at the diner. There's a sign in the window. They're hiring a part-time waitress."

"You've never been a waitress." Arlo couldn't imagine his sister carrying a tray of food. She was strong enough, certainly. She was stronger than most girls her age. But she was clumsy. Back when they used to play tag in the park, she was constantly tripping. She blamed her shoes, but Arlo was pretty sure her feet weren't connected to her brain quite right.

"I can do it," Jaycee said. "And we need the money. So if it comes up, tell mom you don't need me to babysit you."

"I don't!" he exclaimed.

"Exactly."

Their mom came back from the counter with a smile Arlo

hadn't seen in a while. "Good news!" she said. "Your mom just got hired as a waitress. I start tomorrow."

Arlo was careful not to glance at his sister. He didn't need to. He knew the look in her eyes.

Back at the house, Arlo started a load of laundry, careful to make sure the water didn't overflow as the washing machine tub filled up. "One time in twenty, it'll just keep running," Uncle Wade had warned him. "And then the carpet will be squishing for weeks."

Water rose to an inch below the rim, but the machine finally clicked as the valve switched off. Arlo watched as the agitator began churning back and forth. The last peaks of cloth sank beneath the waves.

Arlo's brain felt a lot like his uniform, swirling back and forth, never able to rest. Too many questions were competing for his attention. Who built the trap in the woods? Was it actually meant for Connor? Did someone send the wisps? If so, who? And why? What did it have to do with the girl he had seen in the reflection? Could she actually be Connor's lost cousin? And why was she warning Arlo that he was in danger?

Every time he tried focusing on one question, another one took its place. They were all hopelessly entangled.

Arlo imagined his father facing the same situation. *Every big problem is just a bunch of little problems,* his dad would say. *Doesn't matter if it's making dinner or flying to the moon. You've just got to break it into steps.*

When his father was working, there were whiteboards and index cards and little black notebooks with lists. Arlo didn't really understand what his dad was doing—something about how to tell when someone is eavesdropping on a private conversation—but he understood the process. His father started with complicated things and found ways to make them smaller and easier.

Maybe Arlo could do that.

He didn't have a whiteboard, so he wrote with his finger on the dust of the window:

Wisps?

Cousin?

Then he added a final item:

Why me?

10

THE BESTIARY

ARLO DECIDED TO START WITH THE WISPS.

The Field Book wasn't much help, offering only two short sentences: "Seen at a distance, wisps are often mistaken for lanterns or torches. They may seek to lure unwary travelers into deadly traps."

Based on his encounter, Arlo found this description accurate but unhelpful. It was like saying rocks were heavy and hard and dangerous when thrown at your head.

Arlo wanted to know whether the wisps knew what they were doing when they coaxed him into the woods. Was it planning or instinct? Maybe they were like spiders who race out to grab whatever lands in their web. Or maybe they were smarter, more like lions who stalk their prey and wait for the right moment to attack.

If they were just dumb flying spiders, Arlo could feel confident they weren't trying to kill him specifically. He had just been in the wrong place at the wrong time.

But if they were like lions—or smarter than lions—they might still be stalking him. This time, he would know enough not to follow them into a trap, but it was unnerving to think that something might be out in the woods, watching him. Waiting.

Giving up on the Field Book, Arlo turned to his uncle's encyclopedias, finding the *W* volume holding up a corner of the couch in the living room. The gold-edged pages were thin and stuck together in places. Arlo finally made it to the proper page.

But there was no entry for *Wisp*. It went straight from *Wisdom* to *Wit*.

— • ◆ • —

"We need to look in the bestiary," whispered Indra in class the next morning. "If there's anything about wisps, it'll be there."

At the front of the room, Mrs. Mayes pointedly cleared

her throat. They were supposed to be finishing their math worksheets.

"Sorry, Mrs. Mayes," said Indra with a sweet smile.

Arlo tried to focus on his fractions, but his curiosity wouldn't let him. He watched as their teacher poured the remains of her coffee over the struggling African violet on her desk. While she was rinsing out the mug in the classroom sink, Arlo whispered to Indra, "What's a bestiary?"

"It's a book," answered Indra and Wu together. Wu was sitting in front of Arlo.

All three watched as Mrs. Mayes stared at her mug, silently deliberating whether she wanted more coffee. She checked the clock, surveyed the silent classroom and reached a decision.

She walked out the door.

Wu immediately turned around in his desk. "We can go after lunch, while the second graders have library time."

Indra agreed. "That's perfect."

"Fitzrandolph will be distracted, so we can sneak in behind the counter. She keeps it in a locked drawer, but I've been working on picking locks, so I think I can do it. The question is whether we take it or just photograph the pages we need and put it back before she knows it's gone. Either way, one of you is going to need to be lookout."

Arlo quickly volunteered.

"Or we could just ask to see the book," said Indra.

Wu considered her suggestion, his fingers tracing the air as if planning a series of steps and outcomes. Finally: "I guess that would work, too."

Mrs. Mayes returned to find Wu facing backwards in his seat, talking with Arlo and Indra. It was pretty obvious they weren't working on fractions.

At lunch, they finished quickly and half ran to the library, hoping to get there before the second graders swarmed in.

Mrs. Fitzrandolph, the school librarian, was a kindhearted woman with a collection of hand-knitted sweaters and tartan-plaid skirts. A burbling humidifier sat on the counter next to a figurine of a Scottie dog playing bagpipes.

"Finch? Well, you must be Celeste Bellman's son," she said. Arlo nodded. "I babysat your mother when she was little, not that she needed much supervision. Your uncle, on the other hand . . ." She trailed off, a shrug that went all the way to her fingers.

Arlo hadn't mentioned his uncle to Indra or Wu, deliberately vague about exactly which house he lived in on Green Pass Road.

"We wanted to show Arlo the bestiary," said Indra. "He's never seen one."

"I'm afraid I have the second graders coming in."

"We'll be quick," Indra promised. "He's never seen a faerie beetle, and we want to let him know what to watch out for."

"Well, that is a good idea," said Mrs. Fitzrandolph. Looking to Arlo: "I remember your uncle had a few run-ins with faerie beetles. And stink razors, too."

Flipping through her ring of keys, Mrs. Fitzrandolph reached below the counter to unlock an unseen drawer. Then she placed a well-worn book up on the counter.

Culman's Bestiary of Notable Creatures looked like an old textbook, not much different from the math book they used every day. "I have to keep it back here because if it was on the shelf, children wouldn't read anything else," said Mrs. Fitzrandolph. "Hundreds of years of literature all around us, books on every subject and corner of the world, but all anyone wants to look at is this gruesome little catalog."

Just then, a line of second graders arrived. Arlo always forgot how small and squirmy they were.

"You can have two minutes," Mrs. Fitzrandolph said, moving around the counter to herd the second graders to the reading tables.

Indra quickly flipped through the book, past fascinating drawings of all manner of strange creatures. Arriving at the *W*'s, she slowed her pace until she finally came upon *Wisp*.

Arlo's heart skipped as he saw the illustration. It was a

simple sketch, but it included all the right details: the shadowy skeleton, the inner glow, the faint trail of glowing ash that fell off it. Whoever drew this picture had seen a wisp just as clearly as Arlo had.

He felt his hands sweating from the memory.

Wu read the text out loud, careful to keep his voice low. "'Malevolent spirits of uncertain origin, wisps—also known as Fool's Fire—feed upon the essence of dying creatures, often after luring victims into natural hazards such as quicksand.'"

"Or traps," said Indra. "Like the one you almost fell into."

Wu kept reading. "'Perimeter wards are generally effective but unnecessary, as wisps are unlikely to engage directly. Sometimes summoned and controlled by eldritch spell casters.'"

Arlo felt himself nodding, but then realized: "I don't know what most of that means."

Indra took it on herself to explain, pointing to the relevant words. "*Spirits* means that wisps are like ghosts or phantoms."

"They're not alive," said Wu.

"Well, they sort of are, but they're not alive like people or animals." She stopped herself to clarify. "You do know there are ghosts, right?"

"I do," said Arlo, happy to be caught up on at least one

thing. Arlo reasoned that wisps must be something like Cooper the dog, who existed partially in this world and partially in another. "It says that wisps feed on the energy of dying creatures. So they're like vampires?"

"There are no vampires," said Wu.

"Really?"

"No. That's just in stories."

It seemed strange that Pine Mountain had ghosts without vampires, but Arlo was relieved nevertheless.

Indra returned to the book. "*Wards* are protections," she explained. "A perimeter ward is a circle that spirits can't cross. You don't learn those until Owl, when you get your Elementary Wards patch. There's also Advanced Wards and Abjurations, but that's an elective."

"We should have had a ward around the camp, right?" asked Arlo.

"We did," said Wu. "Don't you remember when we were setting up the tents, Connor went around and stacked up rocks? He was building the ward."

Arlo did remember, but he hadn't asked about it at the time. "So why didn't it work?"

"Because you stepped outside it," said Wu.

Arlo felt foolish, realizing that none of this would have happened if he'd stayed by the tents, or asked why Connor was stacking rocks, or asked more questions in general. He'd been so afraid of seeming stupid that he'd nearly gotten himself killed.

Indra went back to the final sentence in the entry. " 'Sometimes summoned and controlled by eldritch spell casters.' That's what I was saying in the tent. I think someone built that trap with the spikes, and sent the wisps to lure you into it."

"You mean, lure Connor into it," said Wu.

"I guess. Unless they really were meant for Arlo. Think about it: Connor has been camping dozens of times in the woods, and nothing ever went after him. This was Arlo's first time." Indra turned to him. "Can you think of anyone who would want to kill you?"

"No," he said. "I mean, I just got here."

Wu agreed. "It has to be Connor. There's a reason they were targeting him. It's something about his cousin."

Arlo only nodded. He wasn't ready to tell them about the girl in the reflection yet. He wouldn't even know where to begin.

He pointed to the last few words he didn't understand in the book. "What does *eldritch spell caster* mean?"

"*Eldritch* means 'otherworldly,' " said Indra. "Things in the Long Woods are eldritch."

"And a spell caster is anything that casts spells," said Wu. "Like a witch."

"There are witches?" asked Arlo.

Indra kept her voice low so the second graders wouldn't hear. "There are things much worse than witches."

They returned from lunch to find Mrs. Mayes holding a seating chart. One by one, she assigned students to new desks.

Arlo felt a sinking dread. He had a sense how this would turn out.

Indra was placed in the first row, close to the teacher's desk. Wu was two rows back, on the left edge of the room next to the windows.

Arlo was assigned a desk on the right side of the room by the cabinets. Merilee Myers was seated next to him. She scrubbed the stray marks off her new desk with her pink eraser, occasionally holding it up to her nose.

"I love how they smell." She offered it to Arlo. He passed. "Everything has a smell, you know. Even the inside of your nose," she said. "But you can't smell it anymore because you're used to it."

Indra turned back in her seat, looking plaintively at Arlo and Wu. While almost every student had a new spot, their teacher had deliberately moved the three of them as far away as possible from one another. It felt like a great injustice had been done, separating friends.

I have friends, Arlo thought. That sudden realization eclipsed the pain.

During his brief time in Pine Mountain, he had encountered fantastical creatures and mystical powers. He had nearly been killed. But without even noticing it, he had also made two close friends.

That was as unexpected as anything.

11
THE SPLITTER

IN THE LAUNDRY ROOM THAT AFTERNOON, Arlo dragged his finger through *Wisps?* on the dusty window, crossing it off. It felt good to accomplish something, even if the answers he'd gotten raised still more questions.

The next item on the list was *Cousin?* Hearing the hum of a familiar motor, Arlo knew where to start.

"Yeah, I remember when she went missing," said Uncle Wade, hefting another log into the splitter. "Katie Cunningham. Her family's loaded. They own half the mountain."

He pulled the lever and the splitter squealed into motion. The hydraulic arm pushed the log into the wedge, where the wood cracked in half as easily as water against the bow of a ship. Wade then took each half and ran it through again, dividing it into quarters.

"Her family was camping up at Highcross," said Wade. "Sometime in the evening, two of the kids went missing. Katie and her older brother, maybe."

"Her cousin. Connor."

"That's right." Wade kept splitting logs as he spoke. "I went on search parties for the first week or so. They had us in teams of four, and they would assign us a certain area to sweep. Sometimes you'd have dogs if they had some to spare. They had planes and helicopters to check from the air. But how's a kid going to know to signal a plane? After a week, I thought they were probably dead. Maybe a mountain lion had gotten them. When they found the boy alive in Canada, I was surprised. But not too surprised."

"Why not?"

"Well, either they'd been kidnapped, which made sense because of how rich their family was, or they'd somehow wandered out of our forest altogether."

"Into the Long Woods." Arlo said it carefully, not sure how his uncle would react.

"You know about that?" Arlo nodded. Wade shrugged, loading another log. "Never heard the sheriffs or the state search-and-rescue guys talking about it, but everyone in town suspected that's what might have happened, that the kids had somehow crossed into the Long Woods. I know for a fact the Cunninghams paid serious money to bring in shamans and other mystical folks to help out. But best I know they never found anything to prove that's what happened."

Finished with the wood, Uncle Wade shut off the motor on the splitter. Only then did Arlo realize he'd been yelling over it. The quiet was jarring.

"Have you ever been in the Long Woods?"

Wade paused as he took off his work gloves. "Hard to say. Definitely found myself in some unexpected places. But I don't know if it was the Long Woods, proper. From everything I hear, that's a one-way trip. You find yourself in the Long Woods, you're not coming back."

Arlo helped his uncle stack the firewood against the house. The pitch in the bark made his hands sticky. Only when they were nearly finished did Wade say anything more.

"The Cunningham kids—are they in Rangers with you?"

"Connor is my patrol leader. And Christian is the marshal."

"You oughta be careful around the Cunninghams," his uncle said. "I told you they were loaded, right?"

Arlo nodded.

"Nothing wrong with being rich, but it's hard to figure how they got that way. Until about twenty years ago, the

Cunninghams were the same as everyone else, no better or worse off. Then suddenly they had money. I mean, a lot of money. Bought more land, built a brand-new house. No one knew how they could afford it—or why they stayed here. You got that much money, you could live in nicer places than Pine Mountain."

"Where do you think they got the money?" Arlo asked.

Uncle Wade leaned his hand against the wall. "You know Pine Mountain was originally a mining town, right? There used to be gold mines all over, until they went dry. Well, some of those old mines are on Cunningham property."

"You think they found gold?"

"That's what some folks believe. But mining gold is not a quiet thing. If they were doing that, you'd know it. There would be trucks and equipment and slag in the river. No sign of any of that."

"So what do you think it is?"

Wade's voice got quieter. Arlo suspected this was the first time his uncle had shared this theory out loud. "You know how the Long Woods go everywhere? Well, it seems to me they probably go underground as well. Down into the mines. Cunninghams might be doing business with some folks who aren't from our side of things."

"The eldritch," said Arlo, remembering the word from the bestiary.

Wade looked at Arlo, surprised and impressed. "You pick up quick." Arlo smiled. "Let's say it's the eldritch. If the Cunninghams are making deals with those types, it's less surprising that two of the Cunningham kids ended up in the Long Woods."

"You think they were taken."

Uncle Wade shrugged. "Just speculation. But all the same, in the interest of your safety, I suggest you steer clear of the Cunninghams. Best not get caught up in their trouble."

———◆◆◆———

Arlo scrubbed his hands in the kitchen sink, trying to get the sap off. Normal soap was useless. He had to use the green scratchy bar his uncle kept on the windowsill, the one that looked like it was made of boiled frogs and sandpaper. It barely lathered, but it cut through the stickiness.

Scraping with his fingernails, he picked the last bits clean.

That's when he spotted Jaycee outside. She was walking away from the house, up the slope into the forest.

Arlo thought this was strange, because his sister hated nature and exercise. Shaking his hands dry, he decided to follow her.

It was late afternoon, and a cold wind had started to rise. Arlo could hear it in the trees, pine branches swaying overhead. He stayed way back, just barely keeping Jaycee in his sight as she made her way up the slope.

As best he could tell, she was not following any set path, yet she seemed to know where she was going. Arlo wondered if he should duck behind trees and rocks for cover like they did in adventure movies, but there seemed to be no point. Jaycee had no idea he was there.

After a few minutes, Jaycee stopped. Arlo froze, looking for a place to hide. But she didn't look back. Instead, she carefully ducked under a barbed-wire fence and kept walking.

Arlo's heart was beating fast, and it wasn't just from climbing the hill. His sister was crossing onto someone else's property. She was trespassing. Breaking the law.

His first instinct was to run back to the house and tell his mom or Uncle Wade. Jaycee would be in trouble, no doubt. She might get grounded. She would be angry with Arlo for weeks. Still—*You did the right thing, telling me,* his mother would say. He would be protecting the family.

Arlo's second instinct was to follow Jaycee. Wherever his sister was going, she had a purpose. There was something interesting on the other side of the fence. This might be Arlo's only opportunity to see it. And even if he got caught, Jaycee would take most of the blame—after all, he was just following her.

If he followed her. He had to decide.

He thought back to what his mom had said before the first Ranger meeting, how most of the things in life she regretted were things she didn't do, chances she didn't take. Arlo felt a little strange using his mother's advice to justify trespassing, but everything since they'd arrived in Pine Mountain had been a little strange.

Reaching the fence, he carefully slipped between the second and third lines of wire.

As he stood, he felt himself yanked back. Something had grabbed him, choking him.

He gasped with panic. He was about to yell for help, hoping Jaycee would hear him—until he realized that his hood had simply snagged on one of the barbs.

Working blindly with his fingers behind his head, he tried to get himself free. But the barb was like a fishhook caught deep in the fabric. The more he wriggled, the more stuck he became.

Arlo forced himself to stop and think. He silently counted to three. And then he figured out what to do.

He slid out of his sweatshirt, leaving it stuck on the line.

Once he was free, it was simple to get it unsnagged. There were a few small holes, but no serious damage.

He spotted Jaycee just as she was disappearing over the next rise. He scrambled after her.

Once he reached the top, Arlo found his sister standing at the edge of a cliff, wind blowing back her hair. She was preparing to leap to her death.

12

SIGNAL ROCK

"JAYCEE! DON'T!" ARLO YELLED, running across the clearing.

His sister turned around, surprised and annoyed. She had her phone in her hands, typing something.

"Did you follow me!?" she yell-asked, knowing the answer before she finished the question. "You're such a little narc." She hit send on the message she was typing. Her phone bleeped.

As Arlo got closer, he realized the "cliff" was actually just a massive wedge of rock embedded in the hillside. At most it was ten feet above the ground. It looked much higher because the mountain sloped away from it, revealing the whole valley.

Climbing up beside his sister, Arlo could see the town of Pine Mountain below: the flat roof of the school, the church steeples, the gas station sign. Everything looked tiny, like the buildings of a model train set.

"This is the only place I can get a signal," she said, going back to her phone. It bleeped as she got a new message.

"Who are you texting with?" he asked. "People back in Chicago?"

"No. Some girls in marching band."

"Didn't you just see them, like an hour ago?"

"That was at school. A lot happens between four and midnight."

"Like what?"

"I don't know, stuff. Jokes. Plans. There are a bunch of conversations, and if you're not part of them, you get way behind. You're the only one who doesn't know what's going on."

Her phone bleeped again. Arlo looked over Jaycee's shoulder as she typed back an answer.

"What's wrong with mustard?" Arlo asked, confused.

"Nothing."

"Then why did you say, 'It's the worst'?"

"I was just agreeing with her."

"But you love mustard." Arlo had seen his sister put mustard on things that definitely didn't need it, like potato chips.

"It's not about the mustard! It's not about anything. You just have to keep the thread going. If you don't answer back, it dies." Her phone bleeped with various emoji. "You don't understand because you're twelve and you're a boy."

Arlo suspected he did understand, at least to some degree. He thought back to the campfire in Ram's Meadow. Once it was going, it didn't take much supervision. You simply added a log every now and then. The tricky part was getting the fire built in the first place. He remembered how careful Wu was when he lit the tinder, adding sticks of kindling one by one as the flames grew. Wu was methodical and patient, never rushing, never looking away.

Jaycee's new friendships were like a just-started campfire. They needed constant tending or they would die.

"We should call this place Signal Rock," Arlo said. It sounded important and official.

"Fine," she said. "But you can't tell Mom I'm out here, ever."

"I won't." Arlo meant it. In fact, he liked having a secret to share with his sister, something only the two of them knew. But then he added quietly, "I think it's trespassing, though."

"It's fine. This kid in band, I told him where I lived, and he's like, 'Oh, we own the property next to you.' But they don't live here. His family owns, like, half the valley."

Arlo felt a sinking feeling. "Is his last name Cunningham?"

Jaycee was surprised he knew the name. "Yeah, Christian. He's first-chair trumpet."

Arlo didn't explain how he knew the name. Instead, he asked, "Can I use your phone? I want to look something up."

Jaycee glared at him with side-eyes—she had never allowed Arlo to touch her phone. But then she softened, perhaps realizing she needed him to keep the secret of Signal Rock. She handed over the phone. "Two minutes. And don't read any of my messages."

Arlo pulled up the search bar and typed *Katie Cunningham Pine Mountain.*

The results page listed more than eight hundred news stories. He clicked on the top headline, "Local Kids, 4 and 6, Missing Near Highcross." The text loaded first. He skimmed it as quickly as he could.

The article from the *Pine Mountain Gazette* was eight years old. Everything seemed to match up with what he had learned around the campfire and from his uncle: Connor and his younger cousin Katie had wandered away from a family picnic. Rescue patrols from Pine Mountain and across the state were searching the woods.

Arlo clicked another headline, "Missing Colorado Boy Found Alive in Canada." This article from the *Denver Post* described how Connor was found in the Alberta woods a month after he disappeared. Connor's father was quoted, calling it "a miracle" and saying that they held out hope Katie might still be found.

As Arlo was reading, the final image loaded. It was a photo

of Katie Cunningham, age four. She was a preschooler with chubby cheeks and a bow in her hair. Arlo stared at the photo, trying to decide if this could be the same girl he had seen in the window's reflection. That girl was around twelve—*which is how old Katie Cunningham would be now,* he thought.

"Who is that?" asked Jaycee, looking over his shoulder.

"She's Connor's cousin. Christian's too, I guess," he said. "She disappeared."

Jaycee took the phone from him, suddenly intrigued. She skimmed the article, then went back to the search results, scrolling through the headlines. Arlo wanted to keep reading, but knew better than to push his luck.

He saw Jaycee's eyes crinkle. She let out a small "whoa."

"What?" asked Arlo.

Jaycee read aloud from a different article. " 'Detectives leading the investigation into the disappearance of Connor and Katie Cunningham have arrested Wade Bellman . . . ' "

"Is that Uncle Wade?"

She nodded and continued reading: " '. . . of Pine Mountain on charges of tampering with evidence.' "

"What does that mean?"

"I don't know."

"What did he tamper with?"

"It doesn't say." She went back to reading: " 'According to officials, Bellman is not considered a suspect in the children's disappearance. The Cunningham cousins went missing seven days ago from a family picnic near Highcross.'"

"So this was before they found Connor in Canada," said Arlo.

"I guess. It doesn't say what happened, though. A lot of times, people get arrested by mistake. It doesn't mean they did anything wrong."

"Like dad."

"Exactly."

Arlo looked back to their side of the mountain, as if he could see their house. "Do you think Mom knows?"

"She has to, right? I mean, she would know. It's her brother." Jaycee sounded like she was trying to convince herself. "Mom wouldn't bring us here if she didn't think it was safe."

Arlo knew it wasn't safe. There were strange creatures in the woods, and hidden pits with spikes. But this didn't feel like the right moment to bring that up.

"What do we do?" he asked.

"I don't know." Arlo and Jaycee stood on the rock in silence. The sun was just touching the tops of the trees. It would be dark soon.

Jaycee finally spoke. "We shouldn't say anything. Whatever happened, it was years ago. There's nothing we need to worry about now."

Arlo nodded. His sister was right.

Unless she was wrong.

"Can I see one more thing on your phone?" he asked. "Just thirty seconds."

She handed it to him.

He went back to the first article. It had the best photo of Katie Cunningham. He stared at it, trying to mentally add eight years of age to her face, like the missing kids on the backs of milk cartons.

That's when he noticed something.

He turned the phone sideways, zooming in on the photo until the girl's eyes filled the screen.

Like Arlo, young Katie Cunningham had one green eye and one brown eye. *It's just how things are,* his mom always said. *Some people have green eyes and some have brown. You have one of each.*

So did Katie Cunningham.

That couldn't be a coincidence.

—•◦•—

Arlo knew many impossible things.

He knew about wisps and ghost dogs. He had experienced them firsthand.

He also knew about wards and witches—and worse-than-witches—who lived in the Long Woods. It wasn't the same kind of knowing, though. It was secondhand, borrowed. He only knew about them because Indra and Wu had told him. He believed wards and witches were real because he trusted his friends were telling him the truth. But it wasn't the same as seeing them.

Sitting cross-legged on the washing machine, Arlo started sorting through all the facts in his head, tossing them in one of two buckets: *I Saw It* or *Someone Told Me*.

In the *I Saw It* bucket, he put all his memories of growing up: the time he broke his wrist roller-skating, the giant lightning storm in Chicago, finishing the thousand-piece puzzle with his mom. He included the things he had discovered himself, like how mixing one part orange soda with two parts root beer was unexpectedly delicious. He added Signal Rock, snaplights, thunderclaps, and the purple goo on Wu's face. He was certain all of these things existed because he had experienced them himself.

In the *Someone Told Me* bucket, Arlo put most of what he had been taught in school: the state capitals, long division, and how to spell *tomatoes*. It's not that he doubted Boise was the capital of Idaho, but he had never been there to check for himself.

He thought about the disappearance of his sister's jacket, his mom losing her job, and the events that took his father to China. In all three cases, there was no way to know for certain what really happened. He couldn't travel back in time to see for himself. The answers, if there were answers, were not going to come easily.

He looked at the list written on the dusty window. Just hours earlier, he had crossed out the first item (*Wisps?*), but had he really answered the question? *Culman's Bestiary* listed facts about wisps, but couldn't answer why they'd come after him in the first place.

The second item on the list (*Cousin?*) was even less answered. He now knew Katie Cunningham's name and what she looked like, but was she the same girl he had seen reflected in the window? Was her warning ("Be careful, Arlo Finch.") just general advice, like "Don't stick paper clips in electrical sockets," or was it specific to him? How were they even talking? What was their connection? Why did she have the same mismatched eyes as him?

The final item on the list was: *Why me?*

That was the fundamental question, Arlo decided.

As curious as he was to learn about wisps and witches and what had really happened when Katie and Connor disappeared, he mostly wanted to know how it all related to him.

He had been in Pine Mountain less than a week, yet he could already feel things shifting. He wanted to know what would happen next.

Arlo wiped away the words on the dusty window. That's when he saw it.

Snow.

It was falling in large, delicate flakes, each one floating down like a feather. The ground was already covered in a soft layer of white.

Arlo leaned on the windowsill, watching how the snow drifted across the moonlight. For a few minutes, the swirling questions in his head went quiet. He didn't worry about wisps and witches and worse-than-witches.

He simply watched as winter came to Pine Mountain.

13

BLUE BERTHA

ARLO RAN AS FAST AS HE COULD, his boots slipping in the muddy snow.

He could feel his pulse in his ears, his lungs burning in the cold air. But he had to keep running. He had to stay on his feet. One slip and he would be trampled. Crushed.

Wu was right beside him, and faring no better. The yellow plastic rope was sliding through his gloved hands. Worse, his wool cap was inching lower and lower on his face. He shoved it back with his sleeve.

"Keep going!" shouted Connor, right on their heels. Bigger and stronger than the rest of the patrol, he had loops of rope over both shoulders. He was pulling most of the weight.

Ten feet back, Indra and the twins were attempting to

push and steer the hulking blue sled. Indra lost her footing and face-planted in the snow.

Arlo looked up, breathless, squinting in the sun.

It was the first practice for the Alpine Derby sled race, and the other patrols were far ahead, nearing the edge of the snowy church lawn. Red Patrol was the first to reach the halfway mark, a big brick sign with interchangeable plastic letters (THE LORD IS PATIENT, WHY NOT YOU?). They veered right to circle behind it.

Meanwhile, Wu was losing the fight with his hat. It slipped down over his eyes. He was running blind. Arlo grabbed the edge of Wu's jacket, attempting to steer him.

Spitting out snow and grass, Indra raced to catch up with the sled.

Red Patrol emerged from behind the sign. Russell Stokes was pulling the lead. He looked like a sweaty, redheaded ox, each breath fogging the air. The whole patrol had shed their coats before the race started, running in just T-shirts. They were missing a few members—it was basketball season—but that was not slowing them down.

Green Patrol cut wide to circle behind the sign. What they lacked in horsepower, they made up for in technique. They kept a single Ranger at the back of the sled, a tiny girl who was responsible only for steering and shaking a sleigh bell to keep them in rhythm as they sang:

Green Patrol is who we are
Faster than a shooting star
Green Patrol is here to say
Teamwork, teamwork, all the way!

Back at the blue sled, Indra screamed at Julie, "Don't stand on the runners!"

"Don't fall!" Julie shouted back.

"Stop fighting!" yelled Jonas.

Russell Stokes cough-shouted "Losers!" as the Red team raced past, already headed for the finish line.

Wu slowed, trying to fix his hat. Connor nearly ran over him. In frustration, Connor grabbed Wu's hat and tossed it aside. "Keep running!" he shouted.

With a burst of anger and adrenaline, Wu charged ahead. There was no slack in the rope, so he was mostly pulling Arlo and Connor, rather than the sled.

Green Patrol raced past them, smiling as they sang. Arlo grimaced. How could they be so happy? Pulling these sleds was torture.

"Get ready to turn!" shouted Connor. They were approaching the sign.

Arlo had no idea how to turn. Was he supposed to go faster? Slow down? He was on the inside of the "track," closer to the sign. Maybe he was supposed to take shorter steps?

As they passed the sign, Arlo, Wu and Connor veered left. But the sled kept going straight, pure momentum. The trio in back had no idea how to steer it.

Arlo suddenly found himself flying forward like an accidental water-skier. He went face-first into the wet snow, which slid into his parka.

Connor and Wu dug in their heels, yanking with all their might. The giant blue sled tipped on its side, then all the way over. Indra and the twins barely got out of the way as it rolled, cargo spilling everywhere.

Arlo sat up on his knees, wiping the snow out of his eyes.

"We have to steer from the back!" shouted Indra.

"Then steer!" answered Connor, running up to the crashed sled. "Help me flip it."

Arlo staggered over as the patrol got the giant sled set right. They positioned it so they wouldn't need to turn again. Then they salvaged the contents of the sled: one fire barrel, one hatchet, one first aid kit, two pots, three cans of stew, four gallons of water and fifty feet of rope.

By the time they got the sled reloaded, Red Patrol was almost at the finish line.

"It's over. They won," said Wu.

"We have to finish!" said Connor, lashing down the last of the gear. "Everyone pull. I'll push."

The five junior members of the patrol took spots along

the yellow rope, trudging their way back. They weren't even trying to run. They just wanted this to be over.

Arlo watched as Green Patrol finished. They gathered in a tight circle for a final round of their racing song, ending with whoops and clapping. *They're cheering for second place,* he thought. *They'd probably cheer if they came in last.*

Minutes later, when Blue Patrol finally crossed the finish line, there weren't any hugs or high fives. They each walked in their own direction, avoiding eye contact. Wu went back to retrieve his hat.

Christian marked down their time on a clipboard. "All right. So, some patrols have a lot of work to do. Alpine Derby is in eight weeks. You need a plan for getting ready."

The Alpine Derby was the annual winter event in which patrols from around the region gathered to compete in Ranger skills, from pathing to pinereading, rescue to ropecraeft. Patrols raced their sleds to various stations in the wilderness, completing tasks at each one.

Last year, Pine Mountain Company had performed poorly, with no patrols placing in the top five. Blue would have finished last of all twenty patrols, except "this one patrol from Wyoming fell in a river and two of them got hypothermia, so that slowed them down," explained Connor. "But not as much as you'd think."

In order to avoid another disastrous derby, the company had begun practice weeks earlier than usual.

Christian told the patrols to put their sleds back in the storage room. As Russell Stokes was zipping up his jacket, he hissed to Arlo under his breath, "Your patrol sucks."

"You suck," said Arlo, not whispering at all. He wasn't sure why he said it. It didn't seem like him at all. But he was exhausted, and Russell was a jerk.

Christian came up behind him. He had heard the exchange. "Ranger's Vow, right now. Both of you."

Russell knew the drill. He put his fist over his heart and raced through the Vow like he was reciting the alphabet, ending with ". . . forestspiritshearmenowasIspeakmyRanger'sVow."

Christian looked to Arlo—his turn. Arlo had been practicing the Vow, but the words kept getting mixed up. "Loyal, brave, kind and new . . ."

"True," said Christian, correcting him.

True. It was such a strange word in the Vow. A person could be loyal or brave or kind, but how could a person be true? An answer could be true, as in, not false. Arlo wondered if they really meant *truthful* but shortened it so that it would rhyme with the next line.

Perhaps recognizing Arlo's puzzled expression, Christian said, "True like an arrow, how it flies in a straight line. And also, true to yourself."

"Not true like honest?"

"That too. Sort of all of it. There's not a bad way to be true."

Getting the nod from Christian, Russell went back to his patrol, helping them carry their sled inside. Christian stayed with Arlo. "How well do you know the Vow?"

"I've almost got it memorized." (This was not quite true.)

"It's not about memorizing. You have to know it. Really understand it. The only way to do that is to live it."

In a flash, Arlo thought back to his two buckets of knowing. Christian was telling him the Vow needed to be in the *I Saw It* bucket rather than the *Someone Told Me*.

"Okay. Thanks."

"Russell's a jerk, but he's trying to be better. You have to try, too."

"I will." Arlo meant it.

As Christian headed off, Blue Patrol slowly gathered around their hulking sled, which was known throughout the company as Blue Bertha.

No one knew exactly how old Bertha was, but it had been part of the Pine Mountain Company for years, passed from patrol to patrol. It was made of plywood and two-by-fours held together with nails, screws, bailing wire and duct tape. The blue paint was chipping off in places, revealing earlier colors. On the sides, the racing stripes were starting to peel off. Arlo only now realized they were actually just masking tape.

"We're never going to win with Bertha," said Wu. "She's too big and too heavy."

"She's sturdy," said Connor.

Indra agreed with Wu. "You don't need sturdy, you need fast. The Red sled is made of aluminum—"

"And the Green sled is wood," countered Connor. "Ninety percent of Alpine Derby sleds are wood."

"Yeah, but half as much wood," said Wu. "Bertha is like if you made a normal sled and you just kept adding and adding until there was no more wood left in the world. And it's like they found the heaviest wood out there. Ironwood or something."

Jonas sided with Connor. "That's why she's so good. She's indestructible."

"So's a tank. You don't want to push a tank through the forest."

"The problem isn't the sled!" said Connor, almost shouting. "It's us. We need to practice. Green's sled is as old as ours, but they have a rhythm. They're in sync."

"We could be in perfect sync and we'd still be last," argued Indra. "Because we're dragging this awful sled."

Julie finally weighed in. "Maybe if we waxed the skis . . ."

"It's not just the skis. We need to build a new sled," said Wu. Arlo noticed Wu made eye contact with each one of them as he spoke. "This is a race, and in a race, you need the fastest vehicle. That's how you win."

Connor shook his head. "The sprint is only worth ten points. The individual stations are worth just as much—"

Indra interrupted. "But you get extra points based on the order you get back. Bertha isn't just terrible in the sprint. She's terrible everywhere. We get stuck on trails. That costs us time. Plus we're exhausted when we get to the stations because we've been dragging her for so long."

Nothing was going to convince Connor. "We only have eight weeks. We need to focus on skills. We can't waste time arguing about the sled."

Arlo stayed quiet. He wasn't sure he had an opinion.

"I say we vote," said Wu. "All in favor of building a new sled?"

Wu and Indra raised their hands. They both looked at Arlo, gesturing for him to join them. He hesitated.

Luckily, Connor interceded. "I'm the patrol leader. It's my decision. We're not building a new sled."

Indra wasn't backing down. "I'm the patrol quartermaster. Quartermaster is responsible for procuring and maintaining all patrol gear."

"The sled isn't gear. The stuff in the sled is gear."

"I don't think that's right. We should check the Field Book."

Wu tried a new tactic. "I think we should vote on whether we should vote. All in favor of voting?"

"That doesn't make sense," argued Connor. "You can't vote on voting."

"So what, you're king now?" asked Indra. "We don't get to vote on anything anymore?"

"We voted on what to have for dinner last campout," said Julie, trying to be helpful. "We had stew even though I hate stew."

"We know, Julie!" snapped Indra. "You bring it up every time."

"Because I hate it every time."

Connor took a step back. "You want to vote? Fine. Let's vote. All in favor of building a new sled, raise your hand."

Indra and Wu shot their hands in the air. Julie and Jonas shook their heads. They were voting no.

All eyes went to Arlo. He could feel the weight of the stares. He had deliberately stayed out of the argument, but now it was down to him.

"I'm really fine either way," he said.

"You have to vote," said Indra. "Not voting is the same as voting no."

Arlo took a deep breath and let it out slowly. He felt his hand rising in the air beside Indra's and Wu's.

"All opposed?" asked Connor. Julie and Jonas raised their hands. So did Connor. "That's three-three. Motion fails. We're not building a new sled. And that's the last I want to hear about it, understood?"

Wu and Indra exchanged a look, frustrated but resigned.

Twenty minutes later, while Arlo was waiting for his mom to pick him up, Wu and Indra sidled up to him. The trio was alone.

"What are you doing Saturday?" asked Wu.

"I don't know. Homework?"

"Come over to my house. Don't tell anyone else."

"Why?

Indra exchanged a smile with Wu. "We're going to build a new sled."

14
MR. HENHAO

LOYAL. IT WAS THE FIRST WORD in the Ranger's Vow, the kind of term that was easier to understand by example than definition.

Dogs are loyal. Arlo remembered reading about a dog in Japan who waited at the train station every afternoon. Summer or winter, rain or shine, the dog was always ready to walk home with its owner, an old man who worked in the city. Then one day, the old man died while at work. For the rest of its life, the dog would still walk to the station and wait for its master to get off the train. Only when the last train departed would the dog finally head home alone.

Arlo's dad was loyal to the Boston Red Sox, despite not

having lived there since he was a boy. In Chicago, men on the L train sometimes made rude comments about his dad's baseball cap, calling his team worthless or pathetic. "Doesn't matter whether they win or lose," his father told him. "Once you pick a team, you stick with it. It's like marriage—for better or worse, thick and thin." When watching really important games, he would send Arlo to fetch his special red socks for luck, the ones he kept at the back of the drawer and never washed until the end of the season.

Loyalty is also why Arlo voted to build a new sled.

He had no strong opinion either way. He was happy to let Connor make the decision and leave it at that. But Indra and Wu were his best friends, and they were counting on his vote—even if the vote didn't matter in the end. To side with Connor and the twins would have been a betrayal.

Maybe that's loyalty, Arlo thought. *Doing right by your friends when it would be easier not to.* He was like that Japanese dog, or his dad on the L train, enduring minor hardship out of obligation.

Loyalty was not an oath you swore in front of witnesses, or spitting in your hand before you shook to seal the deal. It wasn't a contract. It was just there. Loyalty was a promise you never needed to make.

Now, standing on Wu's snowy porch with his finger

reaching for the doorbell, Arlo was questioning his own loyalty.

Connor had allowed a vote, and the decision was no. Yet here Arlo was, preparing to build a new sled in secret with Indra and Wu. In being loyal to his friends, Arlo was being disloyal to his patrol. He felt like a traitor. Yet sometimes traitors were the actual heroes, because they stood up for what was right when everyone else blindly followed—

"Arlo?" asked Indra. He was surprised to find her standing behind him. Her mom's car was idling on the street. "Are you going to ring or not?"

Arlo hesitated. "I don't know."

Indra reached past him to ring the bell. "I'm so excited. They're going to freak out when they see what we've done."

—◆◆◆—

Wu had planned every detail of the new sled.

"This rack holds our water bottles." His finger traced along a pencil sketch, one of nine drawings spread across the dining room table. "The bottles are color-coded. I made a chart, but we can swap colors if we need to. Figured I should be blue like Wu so it's easy to remember."

He handed Arlo the water bottle color key and pulled forward a different schematic that showed the sled in profile. "Next, aerodynamics. We aren't going to have time for a wind tunnel test, so I went with a basic teardrop shape, which should be good enough. This little ski in the front is for maneuverability. We want a tight turning radius with maximum torque."

"What's torque?" asked Arlo.

"It's good," said Wu. "You want torque. Now for the cargo compartment, I figured we could have detachable pods. So when we get to the Rescue station, for example, we just pop out the part with the first aid kit and go." He pointed to a stripe along the front edge of the sled. "These are actually LEDs. They're like headlights for when it gets dark."

Arlo nodded, impressed.

Indra studied the drawing more closely. "What's the sled made of?"

"So I've been doing some research. For the right combination of high strength and light weight, we'll want to use carbon fiber over a titanium frame."

"Where do we get that?"

Wu was caught off guard by the question. He was so immersed in the design phase he hadn't yet considered construction. "We could probably order it online. Or maybe in

Denver? One of our parents could drive us to a store that sells titanium and carbon fiber. Or maybe they're different stores, I don't know. But I'm sure someone sells it."

"Denver is a six-hour drive," said Indra. "Twelve hours round-trip." Wu nodded, biting his lip. "We need to get the sled built today. By five o'clock. My mom is picking me up then."

"Mine too," said Arlo.

Wu stared at his drawings, hoping that somehow they would provide him with an answer. He rearranged them on the table, then rearranged them again, as if they were puzzle pieces. Finally, he said, "Maybe we could adjust the design a little bit based on what we have."

"What do we have?" asked Arlo.

"We could check the garage."

Except for a small space by the workbench, Wu's garage was packed from the floor to the rafters with boxes, bicycles, baby furniture, two snowmobiles, three lawnmowers, a canoe and a stack of damaged mannequins. "We used them one Christmas as the Three Wise Men," Wu explained. "But a moose ate their hands."

Indra took charge. "Everyone take a section. There's got to be something here we can use."

Arlo chose the area closest to the garage door, figuring that if the piles of junk suddenly collapsed, he would have the best chance of leaping to safety.

He wasn't quite sure what he was looking for, so he decided to focus on eliminating items that were definitely non-sleddy. He quickly ruled out three stacks of astronomy magazines, a miniature pinball machine, several bowling balls and a giant teddy bear with stuffing coming out of its foot.

In one box, Arlo found a taxidermy skunk posed like it was dancing. He wondered if it was Uncle Wade's work, but it wasn't signed on the bottom.

He skipped over a broken table, but then gave it a second look. The three remaining legs were stout, square wooden posts. He could envision them being part of a sled, even if he wasn't sure what function they would serve. With his fingers, he carefully unscrewed the bolts, detaching the legs from the tabletop.

"They don't like it when you do that," said a girl's voice.

Arlo turned to see Merilee Myers standing on the driveway. She was carrying a flute, which she pointed at the disassembled table. "When you take a table's legs, it's basically amputation."

"It was already missing one," said Arlo.

"We had a dog with three legs and it was perfectly happy. But we would never cut off its other legs. That would be unfathomable."

Arlo remembered why he rarely spoke to Merilee in class.

"I live across the street," she said, pointing to a yellow house. "We don't have a television. Our family doesn't believe in it. But we do have a puppet theater. Every summer we put on a play. Sometimes a musical."

"Do you invite the neighbors?"

"No. It's a private show." She looked past Arlo to scope out Indra and Wu. "What are you doing?"

"We're building a new sled for Rangers." He immediately regretted saying it. What if she told Connor or Julie or Jonas?

Merilee's eyes narrowed. "Can I help you?"

Arlo paused, trying to think of a reason to say no. Then, in a flash of inspiration, he said, "We have to do all the work ourselves." Arlo wasn't sure that was actually a rule, but it felt plausible. Merilee nodded.

"Can I play my flute?"

He had used up all his no's. "I guess?"

Tucking her long hair behind her shoulders, Merilee positioned the flute in the curve between her lip and chin. She closed her eyes. Then she began to play. It was a cheerful piece that Arlo had never heard before, or at least didn't remember. Classical music all tended to sound the same to him. But Merilee was clearly very good. He could imagine her playing with an orchestra.

Wu and Indra came over, curious. The three of them stood shoulder to shoulder, watching Merilee play on the driveway. Her fingers clicked on the silver keys. Her breath fogged the cold air. With a final trill, the piece was finished.

The three kids clapped politely. Merilee half curtsied. "That was by Mozart. No one knows where he's buried, but he's probably still there."

Without the music, it was very quiet. Arlo felt he should speak, but had no idea what to say.

"You can keep building your sled," Merilee said. "I'll just play to inspire you. That can't be against the rules, can it?"

With that, she started a new melody, just as lovely as the first. Arlo, Wu and Indra exchanged glances, shrugged, then got back to work.

Wu found a pair of skis by the back wall. They were twenty years old, but still in good shape. Wu felt certain his father wouldn't miss them.

Indra dragged over an old papasan chair. Made of bamboo or some other wood meant to look like it, it was essentially a giant cushioned bowl. The fabric was ripped and water-damaged, but, "I thought we could use the base," she explained. Indeed, the chair's stand seemed ideal, particularly when flipped upside down: light, sturdy and the perfect width. "We could lash ropes across and form a sling to hold our gear in a bag."

Arlo's table legs were the perfect size to attach to Wu's skis. Together they could form the sled's runners. Indra's chair base could sit atop them.

They had the pieces. All that was left to do was assemble them into a sled.

With hammers and screwdrivers, they smashed and pried the bindings off the skis. To attach the table legs to the skis, they debated between steel bolts and a tube of construction adhesive they found on a shelf. They decided to use both.

The glue was the easy part. They squeezed it on in thick, toothpaste-like ribbons.

The bolts were trickier. The drill bit screeched and sparked as it dug into the steel-and-fiberglass ski. The whine was so loud it drowned out Merilee's flute. Eventually, they managed to make two small holes in the bottom of each ski.

The heavy bolts they'd planned on using were far too big, so they settled on smaller wood screws. After a lot of struggle and sore wrists, they managed to get them in.

To strap the papasan-chair base to the runners, they salvaged pieces from an old Erector toy set. Since this was a crucial connection, they decided to use as many nails as possible. Arlo hit his thumb twice. When all sixteen nails were in, the joint felt solid.

Indra had a clear vision for how the webbing would work, so Arlo and Wu just watched as she wove and knotted the scratchy sisal rope around the frame. As she finished the final lash, they stepped back to admire their creation.

The sled was surprisingly beautiful. Compared to Blue Bertha's boxy bulk, this was sleek and rounded. Even Merilee was impressed. She shook the spit out of her flute, the droplets raining down on the sled. "I christen thee Butterflower."

"We're not calling it that," said Wu.

"Definitely not," agreed Indra and Arlo.

All that was left was to actually test it on the snow. They carried it over to the street—it was light enough to lift!—and pointed it in the right direction. Arlo and Wu took their spots on the towlines, while Indra held on to the back edge.

Merilee raised her hat high in the air like the flag at a car race. "Three! Two! One! Go!"

As the hat dropped, they started running. Arlo could hear the skis cutting into the snow behind him, but he barely felt the drag of the sled. Even with half the patrol, they were twice as fast. They passed mailbox after mailbox, racing in a straight line.

Reaching the end of the street, Arlo and Wu stopped. The sled slid gently forward between them, easily stopped.

Red-faced and winded, the three kids screamed with joy. Wu jumped in a snowbank to celebrate. Indra beamed. "Connor's going to have to admit we were right."

Connor shrugged. "It's only fast because it's empty."

They had called the rest of the patrol, inviting them over to see their creation. Julie and Jonas came quickly—they lived just down the street. It took nearly an hour for Connor to arrive. The sun was starting to dip low in the sky. The wind was rising, and the temperature was falling. Even Merilee had gone home.

"Once you get all the gear in, it's not going to be any faster than Bertha. And these ropes"—Connor tugged on Indra's netting—"they won't support the weight anyway. I don't know what's going to break first, the rope or the wood."

Wu's grandfather, a heavyset man with white hair growing out of his ears, watched the discussion from the edge of the driveway. He didn't speak English, but seemed to follow the gist of the conversation. He was eating a bag of crumbly pecan cookies. Little bits were stuck in his beard.

"Why are you so negative?" asked Indra. "A patrol leader is supposed to inspire."

"A patrol leader is supposed to make decisions. That's what I'm doing. I'm deciding that we're sticking with the plan we voted on as a patrol, which was to use Bertha."

"But Bertha's terrible," said Wu.

"Bertha is reliable! She's not going to fall apart on the mountain. We have a hundred pounds of gear to carry, and your little bamboo sled can't do that."

Finished with the cookies, Wu's grandfather handed Arlo the empty bag. He then sat down in the sled. The cargo ropes strained, but held. It easily supported his weight. The old man said something in Chinese. Wu translated: "He wants us to pull him."

Everyone looked at Connor. He sighed, resigned. "Fine. You'll see."

The patrol took their regular positions, with all four boys on the ropes, and both girls in back. Waving his hand, Wu's grandfather shouted something in Chinese that presumably meant "Go!"

The boys pulled. The girls pushed. The sled shuddered, then slipped a bit to the right. But soon enough, they were moving in a straight line. Before they even reached the next mailbox, Arlo realized Connor was right: the sled had seemed fast because it was empty. This time, he could feel the weight of Wu's grandfather behind him. Pulling him was work.

But it wasn't a struggle the way pulling Bertha had been,

fighting for each step. He imagined himself as a dog pulling on the leash. That's how much effort it took, no more, no less. He could do this all day.

He looked over at Wu, then back at Connor and Jonas. Without any planning, all four had fallen into perfect sync—left foot, right foot, left foot, right foot. Back in the sled, Wu's grandfather started clapping to the rhythm. *"Yi! Er! San! Si!"* he shouted, repeating the words again and again.

Wu started a chant to the same rhythm: "I don't know but I been told!"

Arlo listened as the rest of the patrol repeated back, "I don't know but I been told!"

"Mountain lakes are mighty cold."

"Mountain lakes are mighty cold!" All the while, Wu's grandfather kept counting off in Chinese: *"Yi! Er! San! Si!"*

Wu pushed the cadence just a little faster. "If you fall in, you'll get wet!"

This time, Arlo joined in. "If you fall in, you'll get wet!"

"And hy-po-ther-mi-a I bet."

"And hy-po-ther-mi-a I bet."

Connor shouted, "Sound off!" The rest of the patrol shouted back, "One! Two!" They were picking up the pace. "Sound off!" Arlo joined for "Three! Four!" The whole patrol together shouted, "One, two, three, four. One, two—three, four!"

They were nearing the end of the street. "Let's try to circle back!" shouted Connor. "Pullers, slow to half. Pushers, keep the weight on the left ski." Sure enough, the sled began to turn. They were about halfway through the arc when Arlo and Wu ran out of road. They were waist-deep in a snowbank.

"It's okay," said Connor. "There wasn't enough room."

Arlo and Wu waded out of the snow. Together, the four boys pulled the front of the sled while the girls kept it steady. Wu's grandfather stayed put. After all, he was supposed to be cargo.

As they pulled the sled back to Wu's house, Arlo was barely even winded.

Indra and Julie helped Wu's grandfather get out of the sled. He tapped it appreciatively, muttering something in Chinese. He nodded, then slowly made his way back to the house.

"What does *hen hao* mean?" Arlo asked.

"Pretty good," said Wu.

The six members of Blue Patrol stood around the sled, no one wanting to acknowledge the argument from a few minutes before. The tension was unspoken but unresolved. Arlo sensed that at any moment, Indra and Connor would be yelling at each other.

And he would once again have to decide where his loyalties lay.

Connor spoke first. "I say we name this sled Mr. Henhao. And we never tell anyone what it means." Arlo looked around, surveying the reactions, relieved to see excited smiles. "All in favor?"

Every hand went up.

— 15 —
SNOW AND ICE

IN WINTER, IT SNOWED ALMOST EVERY NIGHT in Pine Mountain. Usually just an inch or two, but occasionally enough that powder spilled in over the tops of Arlo's boots.

Jaycee grumbled about having to scrape the snow off the car before school, but Arlo loved it. Sometimes he would pretend to be a sculptor chiseling marble, or a paleontologist carefully brushing away sandstone to reveal a fossilized *Stationyx wagonpithicus*.

His favorite part was when the defrosters finally started melting the ice on the windshield. The plastic blade of his scraper would slide across the water drops until it rammed into some still-frozen sections, breaking them into glassy shards. He had seen videos of special ships that sailed the

Arctic Ocean, cracking the ice so other boats could get through. That's how powerful Arlo felt.

Sometimes Jaycee would let him start the car. It was her job—she was almost old enough to drive anyway—but Arlo would quietly ask her every morning after breakfast while their mom was headed upstairs to get ready for work. He could never predict whether Jaycee would hand him the keys. There was no pattern, no warning. When she declined, it was with a simple shake of the head. Arlo couldn't tell if it was out of spite, or responsibility, or fear of getting caught. When she agreed, the keys came with a shrug that suggested indifference more than sisterly kindness.

This was one of the shrug days. Arlo took the keys and raced to the door.

The air inside the car was sparkly and still, light filtering through the snow on the windshield. He could see his breath. Because of the cold, the sounds were heightened, from the metal scrape of the key in the ignition to the crinkling of the plastic seats. He felt like an astronaut on a spacewalk.

Pushing the clutch all the way to the floor, Arlo turned the key. The engine hammered and whined, struggling. He counted aloud, "One, two, three, four." Suddenly, the station wagon shook to life. Arlo exhaled, then turned all the knobs on the heater to full.

By the time his mom came out, her waitress uniform

under her long coat, the car was toasty and snow-free. "Thank you, guys," she said as they all climbed in, even though Jaycee had done almost nothing.

They dropped Jaycee off at the corner of Wirt Road, where four other high school kids were already waiting for the school bus to Havlick. The boys in letter jackets kept their shoulders hunched against the cold, kicking at clumps of snow. Arlo was pretty sure one of the girls was smoking. She turned away as the station wagon approached, but as they drove off, Arlo watched her in the side mirror. Sure enough, a cigarette came up to her lips.

"Yeah, I see it, too," said his mom, looking down from the rearview mirror. "You know not to smoke, right?" He nodded. "And you know why?"

"Because it's bad for your health and it's illegal?" He watched as the girl receded into the distance.

"I'm not sure it's illegal. Maybe it is. The signs at the store always say it's 'unlawful' to sell to minors. I've always thought that was weird. Why 'unlawful'? We never use that word anywhere else."

"Maybe we could tell her parents. I'm sure Jaycee knows her name."

"We don't know what her parents are like. Maybe they already know."

"Then they're bad parents, aren't they?"

His mom cocked her head, a small grimace. "Maybe they're doing the best they can. It's not easy being a parent. There's no field guide like in Rangers."

"It's a Field Book." He immediately regretted correcting her, and the tone of his voice. "Sorry."

She had already forgiven him. "How's all that going? Any more sled drama?" Arlo smiled, surprised to hear her describe it that way. He told her about the latest practice run with Mr. Henhao, this time with all of their actual gear in the sled rather than Wu's grandfather. "Turns out the water is the heaviest thing, so you need to keep it at the bottom so the sled doesn't get top-heavy. Also the fire barrel is sort of hard to fit in, so we need to figure out—"

His mom's hand pressed against his chest. "Hold on."

She had her foot on the brake, but they were still moving. Sliding. Turning. Arlo could hear the wheels scrunching across the snow. Time slowed as he stopped breathing, simply watching as the hood of the car angled towards the edge of the road.

His mom turned the wheel delicately. *Turn into the slide,* he remembered hearing somewhere. She was doing that. But they were still sliding. Her foot gently tapped the brake. They were still sliding. Every second, every heartbeat, they were inching closer and closer to the steep drop-off on Arlo's side of the—

The road was gone. He could only see trees and sky. "Mom!" He gripped the armrest tight.

"Hold on!" She kept turning the wheel. Kept tapping the brake. Nothing changed. They kept moving in a straight line, right over the edge. Arlo closed his eyes tight. It was quiet.

Until it was loud.

The car slammed down with a crunch of snow and metal. He could hear the wheels straining. Something cracked on the underside of the car. They were still moving, but in a different direction. Arlo felt his weight against the door frame. His cheek was pressed against the cold glass.

"Arlo!"

He opened his eyes to find his mother floating above him. She was still in her seat, held in by her seat belt.

The station wagon had landed on the passenger-side door, like a domino on its edge. Arlo was at the bottom. His mom was at the top, yelling, "Arlo?!"

"I'm okay." He said it instinctively, but he was pretty sure it was true. He could see his feet and his hands. Nothing hurt. Nothing was bleeding. Even the car seemed to be intact, no windows broken, the snow having cushioned the impact. It's just that cars weren't supposed to be on their sides, which made the whole thing so strange. *Like being in space,* he thought, remembering how it had felt when he first got into the car that morning. Snow was covering all the windows again.

"You didn't hit your head? Nothing feels cut or broken?"

"I think I'm fine." He looked around as best he could, only then realizing their predicament: how were they going to get out? His door was pinned to the ground, and the driver's-side door was now the ceiling.

His mom unrolled her window. She tried to crane her head up to look through it, but it was impossible from this angle.

"Honk the horn," he suggested.

"There aren't a lot of people on this road. I think we're going to have to get out by ourselves."

"Try. Please?"

His mom forced a smile. Arlo could see she was about to cry, but she held it in. "Okay. We'll try." She pressed her hand on the horn. The blare was muffled by all the snow around the hood, but Arlo was sure someone would hear it.

"Three in a row, with space between them. It's the universal distress call." He could remember the pictures on the page of the Field Book where he had read about signaling. Three lights, three whistles, three anything was the sign you needed help.

She followed his instructions, pressing the horn in three solid blasts. Arlo could imagine the sound traveling through the valley to the sheriff's station down in Pine Mountain. His mom repeated the pattern.

Suddenly, the car was moving again, sliding further down the mountainside. Arlo screamed. It was just a few inches, but it was terrifying.

They were done waiting for help. "Do you think you can climb up?" she asked. Arlo nodded. "Okay, you're going to have to go first." Anticipating his question: "If I take off my seat belt, I'm going to fall on you. You need to go first. You can do it. I can help you."

Loyal, brave, kind and true . . . Arlo heard the Vow in his head. He needed to be brave.

Reaching up, he found the release button for his seat belt. It was hard to press it from this angle, but by using both thumbs he got it to click. The belt retracted normally. He was free.

He twisted around, trying to find a way to climb up. "Don't stand on the window," his mom said. "Stay on the frame part." That was easy enough to do. The hard part was figuring out the first foothold. "You see where the seat connects there?" She pointed to a steel slider. "Maybe use that. And you can hold on to the shifter."

Arlo carefully put his weight on the door, nervous that any large movement would send the car sliding again.

"You're good," she said. "Now just climb right over me."

She reached down to snag the belt loop of his jeans, helping to hoist him up. He grabbed on to the steering wheel. It twisted as he pulled. Something creaked—the car's wheels were turning. "Don't worry about it. Keep going." He wedged a foot on the center console and took hold of the window frame. As he pulled himself up, he felt his mom pushing his butt.

Arlo's head poked out the window. He looked around like a prairie dog peeking out of its hole.

They weren't that far off the road—it was no more than three feet above him. Arlo could see the slash in the snow where the car had gone over the edge.

"Can you get out?"

"I think so." He braced his right foot on the steering wheel, squeezing up through the window. He got his left knee up on the frame. The driver's-side door was clear of snow, so it was easy enough to move across it, inching closer to the road. The metal crinkled in places. He worried he was making dents.

His mom couldn't see him from this angle. "Are you okay?"

"Fine. I'm going to jump."

"Is it safe?"

Arlo wanted to sound confident. "It's easy." It wasn't. Before he could psych himself out, he did a quick three-count and leaped for the road.

He didn't make it.

He landed facedown in two feet of fine powder. It went up his nose and stuck in his eyelashes. He could feel it melting on the back of his neck.

But he was okay. And he was close. He crawled forward a few feet until he was firmly on the road. He stood up on the packed snow and brushed himself off. His face was flush. His heart was racing.

"Arlo?!" His mom sounded so far away.

"I'm fine! You can climb up now!" From where he was standing, it was hard to see the station wagon. Another car driving by might never have spotted them. They could have been there until spring when the snow melted.

"Okay! I'm coming."

All Arlo could do was wait. He heard various noises from the car, what he presumed was his mom getting out of her seat belt and repositioning herself. Then he saw his backpack fly out of the window, landing on the door of the station wagon. His mom popped up after it. He had never been so happy to see her.

"Take your bag." She tossed it to him, then continued to climb out, sitting on the door frame. She paused, catching her breath. Her legs were still dangling in the car, like she was sitting on the edge of a swimming pool.

"Mom?" She looked back at him. "What happened?"

She shrugged. "Sometimes the roads are just slick. And

these tires aren't great. This isn't a great car, to be honest. I'm amazed it's lasted as long as it has."

"Can we fix it?"

"I don't know. I don't know how we'll afford it. But we'll figure it out."

"The important thing is we're okay," said Arlo.

"Exactly." She brushed at the corners of her eyes. Suddenly, a new thought—she patted down her parka, finding her phone. "Here, catch." She tossed him the phone. He caught it, pressing it to his chest.

"Who do you want me to call?"

"No one. Take a picture."

"Why?"

"We'll want to remember this," she said. "Plus, without the photo, who's going to believe it?"

Arlo pulled off his gloves. Unlocking her phone, he switched it to camera. He framed the shot, waiting for his mom to fix her hair. "Okay, ready." She smiled broadly, looking directly at him.

He took the photo.

His mom was right. It helped him remember the moment, and what happened next.

16

THE ROAD

ARLO'S MOM WAS FINISHING HER PHONE CALL. "Exactly. About halfway between Wirt Road and Main Street. Okay. Mitch, thank you so much." She hung up. "The tow truck will be here in half an hour, maybe forty-five minutes."

Arlo peered over the edge at the station wagon. It looked like a discarded toy. "How will they even get it out?"

"I don't know. But they'll have a way. Cars go off the road all the time here." She checked her watch. "Do you think you can walk the rest of the way to school? It's only about a mile. Straight ahead, then left on Main. You know the way."

He nodded. He knew the way, but he wasn't sure it was a good idea. A lot could happen in a mile.

"You have a test in math, right? You don't want to miss that."

In fact, he would have been happy to miss the test, but that wasn't why he was stalling. He didn't want to leave his mom alone here. What if the tow truck never showed up? What if her phone battery died? What if a bear came out of the woods? She hadn't read the Field Book. She wouldn't know how to tell a black bear from a grizzly, whether to back away slowly or shout and make noise. If Arlo left, she was as good as—

"Go. You'll be fine. I used to walk to school."

"In the winter?"

"No. But I already got you halfway there. It evens out." She pulled him in for a tight hug and kissed the top of his hat. "Go. I love you."

"Love you." Arlo put on his backpack.

"And hey, if anyone doubts you, remember," she said, holding up her phone. "We have photographic evidence."

Arlo forced a smile.

The road was quiet. All he could hear was the squeaky crunch of his boots.

At least one car had been down this road today. Arlo walked between the tire tracks, noticing the diamond patterns in the tread. Here and there, a clump of dirty snow would obscure the design. He decided these were likely accumulated blobs that stuck to the wheel well and fell off when they got too big.

He had only been walking a few minutes when it began to snow. The flakes were fine and crystalline, almost like sand. They didn't stick to his gloves or parka, but they wiggled in beneath his collar. He put up his hood for protection.

Crunch crunch, crunch crunch. He kept walking.

Main Street had to be close, maybe just around the next bend.

But it was strange: he didn't seem to be getting any closer to the curve. He was walking towards it, but it seemed to be receding at the same pace, as if the road were somehow stretching in the middle.

Arlo stopped. The bend in the road was exactly where it should be. This was puzzling.

Then he heard a whispering voice, so faint it might have been the wind. It seemed to be calling out to him: "Too-ble!"

He scanned the forest, looking for the source. He spotted crows in the trees. They appeared to be watching him. Could he have mistaken their caws?

"Too-ble!" It was an old woman's voice, low and raspy. It seemed to emanate from the dark woods on his left.

Arlo started walking again. Almost imperceptibly, the bend moved away from him.

"Tooble!" Louder. Closer. He could hear a smile in the woman's voice.

He started jogging, then running, his backpack swinging from side to side. He was definitely moving forward. It wasn't like he was on a treadmill—he was passing trees to his right and left. But the bend was always just as far ahead, no matter how much he ran.

He stopped. His lungs were aching. He could feel his pulse in his ears.

That's when he noticed something else strange. He had been so focused on what was ahead of him that he'd missed what was right at his feet: the tire tracks had disappeared.

On a road with nowhere to turn, where had they gone?

Arlo turned to look back. That's when he saw her.

A girl about his age was standing in the road, twenty feet away, her back to him. Her hair was done up in complicated braids with tiny flowers and sparkling gems. She wore a dress with intricate red-and-gold patterns, but no shoes. She was barefoot in the snow.

Arlo couldn't see her face, but he was pretty sure he knew who she was. "Hello?"

Her head cocked to the side, as if she was confused where the sound was coming from.

"Are you okay?" he asked.

She didn't answer, but her left hand went up beside her, feeling the air. She had rings on her fingers, with golden jewels.

Arlo took a few steps towards her. She didn't react. She didn't seem to hear his footsteps. He ultimately ended up right behind her, close enough that he could have touched her.

Her hand went down. Finally, she spoke. "Is that you?"

"Yes."

"Arlo Finch." Her voice seemed to be coming from all directions. But it was definitely a girl's voice, not the raspy whisper from the forest.

Arlo started to circle her, but no matter which way he moved, her back was always to him. It was like an optical illusion, except he was in the middle of it. He stopped, a little dizzy.

"Are you Katie Cunningham?"

The question seemed to annoy her. "That hasn't been my name for a long time."

"What's your name now?"

"Rielle." Faint music played as she spoke it, as if her name wasn't made of letters but of notes, plucked on strings and played on tiny bells.

"I know your cousin, Connor. We're in Rangers together. He's my patrol leader." She didn't answer. "Do you remember him?"

"Yes."

"Were you kidnapped?"

Another pause. She shook her head. "No. I didn't belong in your world. My place is in the Realm."

"What's the Realm?"

"The eldritch lands. The other side of the Long Woods."

Arlo was confused. He thought the Long Woods *was* the other world. Was she saying that there was a third place? And if that was called the Realm . . . "Then what are the Long Woods?"

"Where the two lands meet." The way she moved her arms, Arlo suspected she was trying to show the intersection with her hands.

"Is that where we are now? The Long Woods?"

"I don't think so," she said. "It's different."

"I'm on a road in the forest. In Pine Mountain. It's snowing here." It seemed odd to have to tell her that, considering she was standing barefoot in the snow.

"It's autumn here," she said. "It's always autumn."

Arlo tried to picture what she meant. People said it was always summer in Phoenix or Mexico because it was warm and never snowed. But how could it always be autumn? Once trees lose their leaves, they don't grow them again until spring.

She continued: "I was walking in the garden, and the path kept shifting. Then I heard a voice. An old woman."

"I heard it, too!"

"She's dangerous. You have to stay away from her."

"Why? What does she want?"

"She wants you."

Suddenly, Arlo felt dizzy again, the world swirling around him. Rielle was walking and he was caught in her wake. He rushed to catch up with her, but each footstep was heavy. "Wait! Why does she want me?"

She stopped. As she turned, she was suddenly behind him. She held his arm tightly as she whispered into his ear: "Because you don't belong in this world either."

As he turned to face her, she was gone.

Arlo Finch was standing alone on the road, the real road, between two tire tracks in the snow. The only footprints were his own.

— 17 —

9:45 A.M.

ARLO DECIDED TO TELL WU AND INDRA EVERYTHING.

During morning recess, the trio huddled beside the snowy monkey bars. Indra listened carefully, mentally taking notes, while Wu paced and broke off icicles. He was paying attention but couldn't focus unless he was doing something with his hands.

Arlo started by recounting his first brief conversation with the girl's reflection in the window, and her vague warning that he was in danger.

Indra stopped him. "You think the wisps were after you, not Connor."

"I guess. But Connor is definitely part of it, too. I'm pretty sure the girl is Connor's cousin, the one who disappeared when they were little." Wu let out a soft "whoa," his mind blown. Arlo explained how he had looked up photos of young Katie Cunningham on his sister's phone. While he couldn't be certain it was the same girl he had seen in the reflection, she had his same mismatched eyes.

Indra stopped him again, as if only she could put the pieces together. "So little Connor and little Katie disappear. They end up in the Long Woods. Connor makes it out somehow, but Katie stays behind. And she's been there the whole time."

Wu held up an icicle like a sword. "We have to rescue her."

"No," said Arlo. "She's not in the Long Woods. She's in the Realm."

"What's the Realm?"

"I'm going to tell you, but you keep interrupting."

Indra huffed. "Fine. Explain faster."

Arlo talked through the events of that morning, starting with the car accident. The details of the crash were so vivid and exciting that he wanted to spend more time on them—he could have died, after all—but those ultimately weren't as important as what had happened on the road. He described the crystalline snow, the voice in the woods, the disappearing tire tracks and how he could never quite reach the bend in the distance.

"That's how it happens," said Indra, interrupting again. "I've read stories about it, people who accidentally cross into the Long Woods . . ."

"He said she wasn't in the Long Woods," said Wu.

Arlo tried to clarify. "Wherever we were, she got there by accident, too. She lives in the Realm."

"You still haven't explained what that is."

"Because you keep interrupting me."

"You need to stop letting me interrupt you!" Indra crossed her arms, annoyed.

Arlo continued, describing the dizziness he felt when he tried to approach the girl on the road. He couldn't remember exactly what each of them had said, but he summarized as best he could. Indra fought her urge to jump in for clarification on each little point, but it was clearly a strain. "I asked her if she was Katie Cunningham. She said her name wasn't Katie anymore. It was Rielle."

"How do you spell—"

Wu shushed her. Indra grimaced, filing the question away for later.

Finally, Arlo explained the Realm to the degree he understood it. "I think there's our world," he said, holding out his left hand. "And there's the Realm." He put his right hand next to it. "And where they touch, that's the Long Woods. It's like the border between the two worlds."

The recess bell rang. They needed to go in soon.

"So what do we do now?" asked Wu. "We have to tell Connor, right?"

Arlo wasn't so sure. "She didn't really react when I said his name. It was like she knew who he was but wasn't all that worried about him."

"Yeah, because Connor's fine," said Wu. "She's the one in trouble."

Indra shook her head. "She could have told Arlo to pass along a message. Like that she's alive. It's weird that she didn't."

"Maybe she couldn't!" said Wu. "Maybe she didn't want Connor to be in danger. They were both kidnapped, after all."

Indra held up a finger to correct him. "She said she wasn't kidnapped."

"Like she knows! She was a stupid little kid when it happened. This girl Katie—or Rielle, whatever—she is trapped in this other world, the Realm. Someone has to go save her."

"Who? Us?"

"Maybe!"

"How?"

"I don't know! We'll figure something out."

"Typical," said Indra. "It's like the sled all over again. Wild plans with no basis in reality."

"The sled turned out great!"

"Yes, because someone—me!—was able to think about it practically."

Arlo realized he hadn't spoken in quite a while. He'd simply been watching them argue, like it was a tennis match on TV. "I don't think Rielle wants to be saved," he said. "She was mostly warning me to stay away."

"Exactly!" said Wu. "Because it's dangerous. She's in danger. When someone's in danger, you save them. That's like basic Rangers."

"It's not at all like that," said Indra. "Let's say someone falls through the ice—"

"You save them!"

"But you don't just run out onto the ice, because the ice could break, and then you're in the water, too. You have to move slowly. You inch across the ice on your stomach, then you throw them a rope. Or better yet, slide a ladder slowly across the ice."

Wu was exasperated. "Remind me never to go ice fishing with you. You'd let me drown while you're flipping through your Field Book to find the right page."

"It's page one forty-eight!"

Arlo looked around the playground. All the other kids had gone in. Another minute and Mrs. Mayes would give them detention.

"I'm going to tell Connor," he said. "Tonight, after Rangers." Wu and Indra looked over at him, surprised that he had come to a decision without them. "I don't know what the right thing to do is. But Connor deserves to know."

— 18 —
KNOTS

"THE RABBIT GOES OUT OF THE HOLE, around the tree, then back in the hole."

Connor pulled the rope tight, showing the completed bowline knot. It looked exactly like the illustration in the Field Book.

Arlo followed Connor's instructions, looping the rope to make a "tree" and a "hole," then using the free end of the rope as the "rabbit" to circle out and back in. He pulled on it, but all he got was a tangle.

"The tree has to grow out of the ground," explained Connor, demonstrating which side of the loop needed to be on top. Arlo tried it again. This time, it worked. The knot was strong.

They were prepping for the knot relay, a race between patrols to see who could tie all ten Ranger knots first. Knots were always one of the Alpine Derby stations, so the company spent a lot of time making sure every Ranger knew them.

Having only just started ropecraeft ("There's an extra *e*," explained Indra. "It's silent but it's important."), Arlo knew he was a liability to Blue Patrol. He was slower than the others at tying the knots, and more likely to mess one up.

Plus he only knew eight of the ten knots.

He felt confident with his square knot, taut-line, clove hitch, sheet bend, timber hitch and two half hitches (which was a single knot, despite the name). He hoped he could remember the bowline and the blood knot. But—

"If he draws a sheepshank or a zeppelin bend, we're toast," said Indra.

The patrols were gathered in their respective corners of the church basement. Some Rangers were stretching their legs for the sprint. Arlo was so worried about his knots that he hadn't even considered the running part. He imitated their stretches, though he wasn't quite sure which muscles he wanted looser.

"Remember, taut-line has two inside the loop, one outside," said Wu. "And sheet bend goes up, around, then tuck under."

"Why is it called a sheet bend?"

"It's good for tying sheets together," explained Indra. "Like if you had to make a rope."

Arlo sparked—that was exactly the knot he needed for escaping from his bedroom in the event of a rockslide! He was about to ask what a sheepshank was for when Christian blew the assembly whistle. It was time to line up.

With six Rangers and ten knots, almost everyone in Blue Patrol would need to go twice. Connor put Arlo at the back of the line. "That way, you'll only have to go once." Arlo nodded, relieved.

He counted Rangers in the other patrols, figuring out who he would be racing against. In Green Patrol, it was a girl named Zaylin. In Red Patrol, it was Russell Stokes. The red-headed brute saw him staring and made wild eyes back at him.

Senior Patrol would be serving as judges. Each took a station at the far end of the room, with a stack of index cards and a three-foot-long rope at their feet.

"Rangers ready!" called Christian. "Set! Race!"

The patrol leaders took the first leg, sprinting across the room to flip a card revealing which knot they had to tie. Patrols cheered as the racers set to work.

Connor was the first to get a thumbs-up from the judge. He sprinted back and handed off the rope to Indra. They were neck and neck with Red Patrol. Green seemed to be struggling, but Arlo wondered if they had drawn a tougher knot to start.

As racers returned, they called out what knot they had drawn.

"Timber hitch," said Connor.

"Sheet bend," said Indra.

"Clove hitch," said Wu.

"Bowline," said Jonas as he handed off the rope to his sister.

In the first four legs, Blue had drawn almost all of Arlo's good knots. Now at the front of the line, Arlo hoped Julie drew a difficult one, saving something simple for him. He watched as she flipped her card, then knelt down to tie a knot around the judge's ankle.

"She's got the taut-line hitch," said Wu.

"That means you're either blood knot, square, sheepshank, or zeppelin," said Indra. Arlo only knew the first two of those. "What if I can't do it?"

"We're dead," said Wu.

Connor took Arlo by the shoulders. "We're in the lead. Just try to tie it right the first time, even if you have to slow down."

Julie got the thumbs-up from the judge and began untying her knot. Arlo felt his pulse quickening with anticipation. Julie was sprinting back. Once the rope hit Arlo's hand, his feet took over. He found himself in front of the judge, flipping the next card.

But there wasn't a word written on it, only a series of squiggles.

Arlo blinked hard, trying to get his eyes to focus. But the lines on the card didn't form letters, at least not in any alphabet he had ever seen. While he was staring at it, Russell Stokes arrived at the station next to him. Red Patrol had caught up.

Arlo turned the card over to show it to the judge.

"Gajn herodut," said the judge. The words were completely foreign to him, and felt like they were sung rather than spoken.

Now doubly confused, Arlo looked at the card again. The squiggles were still just squiggles.

The knot he knew how to tie best was the square knot. So he tied it. He took both ends of the rope, tying them right over left, left over right. He pulled it tight and showed it to the judge.

Thumbs-up. Arlo worked the knot open and raced back to his team, handing the rope to Connor for his second run. He had beaten Russell by two seconds at least.

Wu and Indra gave Arlo high fives as he returned to his place in line. Russell glared over at him. "Emmn sarup. Isthinu talabritic?"

Arlo could tell by the tone it was an insult, but had no idea what the words actually meant. "Baru sledith," he answered.

It felt like his brain had switched to a different language

by accident, like when his dad's computer would show Chinese rather than English. Somehow, the settings in Arlo's brain had gotten messed up.

Arlo looked around the room in bemused wonder, noticing all the small details that had changed. Over the door, there was an illuminated green sign. But instead of the word EXIT, it showed a jumble of random shapes. On the far wall was a large poster with the Ranger's Vow, except the letters were all wrong.

But they were also familiar. He had seen them before, yet couldn't remember where. What's more, he felt like he might be able to understand the writing if he just squinted his mind a little bit. He started to concentrate, blocking out the sound of the cheering Rangers. He began recognizing repeating patterns in the shapes, and how they formed words. He thought he was close to understanding it when—

Wu and Indra grabbed him, cheering.

Jonas had just made it back with the rope. Blue Patrol had won the race, coming in a few seconds ahead of Red. Green was a distant third.

"So glad you got the square knot," said Wu.

"Me too."

Arlo looked back over at the Ranger's Vow on the wall. It was back to being English.

It was always English, Arlo thought. Whatever had changed

wasn't the poster, but his brain. For a few moments, he had forgotten English altogether. He wondered if this explained why he sometimes had a difficult time reading: *Was his brain trying to use the wrong language?*

Which raised the question: What language was it using? Could it have been eldritch? Was that even a language, and if so, why would he know it?

⸻ ◆ ⸻

"What's up? Is this about the sled again? Don't tell me you built another one."

Arlo, Indra and Wu had asked Connor to stay after the meeting. The basement meeting hall was almost empty, just a few Senior Patrol members doing inventory of the quartermaster's closet.

"Arlo has something to tell you," said Indra.

Suddenly on the spot, Arlo wasn't sure where to begin. Should he ease into it gently? *Hey, so remember when you were a kid and disappeared in the woods?* Should he go right to the headlines? *Your cousin is alive in another world, but has a different name and doesn't seem to really care whether you know or not.* He decided to split the difference. "I saw your cousin, Katie. This morning before school. And once before that."

Arlo watched for a reaction. He saw Connor's eyes dip, as if pulling up an image in his brain. His lips moved, as if about to form a word. Then his shoulders went back. His head cocked. "Where?"

"The first time, in a reflection in my room. The second time, on the road coming into town, except it wasn't the road. It was probably the Long Woods."

Connor glanced over to the other Rangers, making sure they couldn't hear the conversation. One of them was his brother, Christian. "How did you get there?"

"I don't really know."

"How did you get back?"

"I don't know that either."

"And you're sure it was her?"

"Yes. I talked with her."

Connor nodded, thinking. "What did she say her name was now?"

Arlo hesitated. He was pretty sure this was a test. Connor knew the name; he wanted to make sure Arlo was telling the truth.

Indra interrupted, pointing at Connor. "How did you know she was alive?"

Connor ignored her. "What's her name now?"

"Rielle," said Arlo.

Connor sighed and ran his hand through his hair. Wu, Indra and Arlo exchanged a look, not sure whether this was going well or terribly.

Connor looked Arlo straight in the eye. "What did she say, exactly?"

"Not much. We mostly talked about how we were talking. I think she was as surprised as I was."

Connor shook his head. "Don't be so sure. You can't necessarily trust her."

"Back up," said Wu. "How did you know she was alive and had a new name?"

"She comes back twice a year to see her parents. Once at Christmas, once at Midsummer. That was the agreement they made."

"With who?" asked Wu.

"The people she lives with now. The eldritch."

It took Arlo a few moments for his brain to catch up. This girl he'd assumed was missing wasn't missing at all. Her family knew exactly where she was. "She said she lives in the Realm."

"I don't know what you call it, but yeah. The place beyond the Long Woods."

Indra jumped in. "So when you guys were kids, and the two of you got lost at Highcross . . ."

"They only wanted her, so they let me go. I really don't

172

remember any of it. They wiped my memory or something."
Arlo was inclined to believe him. Connor seemed both confused by exactly what had happened, and resigned to never knowing.

"Why hasn't anyone tried to rescue her?" asked Wu.

"Some people tried at first." Connor looked over at Arlo. "Like your uncle."

"Uncle Wade tried to save her?"

"You have an uncle?" asked Wu.

Indra suddenly put it together. "The guy who stuffs animals—that's your uncle, isn't it?"

Arlo nodded, but didn't want to get off track. "I read that they arrested him for tampering with evidence."

"He and some other guy were trying to find us," said Connor. "But by that point, my family was already talking with the eldritch. They made a deal: Katie would stay and I'd go home. Part of the agreement was that everything would be kept secret."

"That's why you never talk about it," said Indra.

"And why you can't tell anyone. Not your parents, not Jonas and Julie. If anyone ever finds out . . ." He trailed off. Arlo suspected Connor didn't know the exact details of the deal, and didn't want to.

"Wait, no. Uh-uh." Wu stepped forward. "Your family handed over your cousin to a bunch of weirdos in another dimension, and we're supposed to just shut up and not mention it?"

"She's better off there, seriously," Connor said. "It's like if you had a wolf and you put it in a cage. It could survive, probably, but it doesn't belong there. It needs to be out in the woods. Katie was always strange, even when she was four. She heard voices. She spoke a different language, wrote a different alphabet."

Eldritch, thought Arlo.

Connor continued. "Back then, they thought there was something wrong with her, but . . ."

"She was one of them," said Indra.

"No, not really. That's the thing: she's not one of them either. They need her for something. She's special somehow."

"Arlo must be special, too," said Wu.

Indra agreed. "That's why the wisps showed up at the campout. Whoever sent them was after Arlo."

Arlo felt his stomach tying in knots. He was back to the final question he had written on the laundry room window: *Why me?* "If I'm special, then why would someone try to kill me?"

"I don't know," said Connor. "Maybe they think you're a threat."

— 19 —
TWO DINNERS AND A SNACK

ARLO SPENT THE NEXT FEW WEEKS waiting for something terrible to happen. He knew he had to be vigilant, because someone, somewhere wanted him dead.

Every morning, he would wake up before his alarm, staring at the ceiling while he contemplated how it might happen.

He was pretty sure they wouldn't send wisps again. Indra made a list of other supernatural creatures she thought might be assigned to kill him, ranging from flying wolves to shadow snakes to ear spiders. After a look through *Culman's Bestiary*, he started sleeping with a cotton ball in each ear, just to be safe. He wasn't sure that would actually stop a swarm of hungry ear spiders, but it might slow them down on the way to eating his brain.

Using the knots he'd learned, Arlo fashioned a rope long enough to stretch from his window to the ground. He stored it in the bottom desk drawer and practiced quickly attaching it to the radiator. He figured he could get out in less than twenty seconds if he had to.

But one morning as he stared at the ceiling, Arlo realized how unlikely it was that a creature would be sent to murder him in his home. Like the disappearance of Connor and Katie, a mysterious death would be too remarkable, too newsworthy.

Indra agreed. "Whoever is trying to kill you wants to do it quietly. That's why they sent the wisps the first time. It would have looked like an accident. Like you stumbled into an old hunting trap."

They discussed the various possibilities around the campfire, sitting on benches made of packed snow. Jonas and Julie were away for their grandfather's funeral in Tucson, so the four remaining patrol members could talk openly.

This was the last campout before the Alpine Derby, and Connor had been extra careful when placing the wards around Blue Patrol's campsite. Wu and Indra vowed to never leave Arlo alone in the woods where he could be snatched or eaten. Not that they thought it likely.

"If I was trying to kill you, I'd do it from the inside," said Wu. "I'd get one of your friends or family to do it."

"Maybe use a hex," suggested Connor. "Any witch could do that. Plus there are toads that have mind control."

"If you're going to do that, why not just use a doppelgänger?" Indra explained that a doppelgänger was a faceless shape-shifter who could assume the identity of any person. "For all you know, one of us could be a doppelgänger, just waiting for you to fall asleep so we can smother you." Reading his reaction, Indra quickly added, "We're not, though. We're on your side."

"Definitely," said Wu.

"One hundred percent."

Arlo believed them. Plus he was pretty sure who the doppelgänger might be.

Jaycee had begun acting very strangely. Arlo had seen her smiling for no reason while drying the dishes, a dreamy look in her eyes. She said thank you when Uncle Wade passed the macaroni and cheese, even while their mom was out of the room and couldn't hear it. She took long showers, shaved her legs and began wrapping her head in a towel like they do in movies.

Once, Arlo swore he heard her humming.

This was not his sister. Arlo was pretty sure it was a doppelgänger attempting to act like a "normal" teenager, not realizing that the real Jaycee was incredibly moody and cold, so grumpy she would scoff at rainbows and look away.

At the very minimum, Jaycee was hexed or being controlled by a supernatural toad.

A few days after the campout, Arlo found his sister using the telephone, the old-fashioned one in the kitchen. True, the snow was too deep to hike out to Signal Rock, but it seemed very unlikely that Jaycee would consent to using Uncle Wade's weird wired phone that smelled like burning plastic. But there she was, sitting on the counter, twisting the cord around her finger as she talked.

Arlo tried to eavesdrop as he got himself a slice of cheese from the fridge. But Jaycee wasn't actually saying anything. It was all "yeah"s and "uh-huh"s and "stop!" said with a giggle and a smile.

This was definitely not his sister.

He wanted to tell his mother his suspicions, but she was acting strangely, too. Ever since the car accident, she seemed noticeably happier. Which was odd, because things were worse than ever.

The station wagon needed thousands of dollars of repairs—money they didn't have. Luckily, Mitch, the man who owned the repair shop, had been friends with Arlo's mom back in high school. He'd agreed to do the work in exchange for help with the bookkeeping. "You wouldn't believe how bad his files are," said Arlo's mom. "He has invoices just wedged in a drawer."

Arlo didn't know what invoices were, but his mom did, because she had been an accountant back in Chicago before she lost it and threw a chair at a window. Or through a window. He was still unclear on the details. Bookkeeping apparently combined the worst parts of math and matching socks on laundry day. His mother seemed unaware of how tedious and terrible it was.

"Oh, it's not so bad. I like numbers. And it's nice to be able to help someone," she said, stacking repair-shop paperwork on the dining room table. "I used to double-check Mitch's algebra back in high school. He was always so good with machines, but numbers just never clicked with him."

"Dad is good at machines, too," said Arlo. "Like computers."

"Absolutely!" She searched the table for the right pile for the paper in her hand. "But computers are a different kind of machine. It's really more math than mechanics. But yes, your dad is very smart. A genius, in fact. You know that, right? For what he does, cryptography, he's one of the smartest people on the planet."

Arlo nodded. "Remember when he was building that desk from IKEA, and there were all those pieces, and he couldn't figure out how it went together?"

"Yeah, that took a while. And it still kind of wobbled afterwards." She found the proper stack. "No one's good at everything. And that's how it should be. It gives us a reason to ask for help."

Arlo saw that as an opening to discuss his suspicions. "I think something's wrong with Jaycee. She's acting really weird."

"So you noticed, too." His mom lowered her voice, even though Jaycee was in the kitchen and couldn't hear them. "I don't have confirmation yet, but I'm pretty sure I know what's going on." Arlo nodded, ready for the worst. "I think your sister has a boyfriend."

Arlo knew this was impossible. In order for Jaycee to have a boyfriend, she would have to be someone's girlfriend, and no boy would ever date her. She was surly and short-tempered. She hated dresses and movies and flowers. There's only one way someone would agree to go out with her.

"He hasn't met her yet, has he? It's one of those internet things where he's trying to steal her money." Arlo almost felt bad for the guy, because they had no money to take. Plus he had to talk to Jaycee and pretend to like her.

His mom smiled. "His name is Benjy. I think he plays cymbals in marching band."

"So he's real?"

"I think so. I don't want to pressure her, but I'll ask if he wants to come over for dinner sometime."

Five days later, Arlo was sitting across from Benjy Weeks. He was Jaycee's age, but an inch shorter, with hair that kept getting in his eyes. Other than some acne, there didn't seem to be anything deeply broken about him. He was polite and attentive, even when Uncle Wade went on a long tirade about the US banking system.

Arlo's uncle had just received a large taxidermy order for a ski resort in Jackson Hole ("It's a mountain! Don't know why they call it otherwise."). The payment had to be held at the bank for several days before the money was released. " 'Oh, sir, for amounts of this size it's really better to use a wire transfer than a check.' Can you believe that, Benjy?"

The boy wasn't sure which answer Wade wanted. "No?"

"Well, that's what they told me. They'd rather have a bunch of random numbers than an honest-to-gosh check. You ask me, I blame video games. Most of them don't even have cartridges anymore. How do you know you have something if there's nothing to put on a shelf?" Again, it didn't seem like an answerable question. "And don't get me started on movies."

Everyone carefully avoided getting him started on movies.

At one point, after dinner and before dessert, Arlo was pretty sure Jaycee and Benjy were holding hands under the table.

"Why do they do that?" asked Wu over cookies at Indra's house the next day. "What's so great about hands? They're sweaty and gross."

"Not everyone's hands are sweaty," said Indra, moving the cookies away from him. "There's probably something wrong with you."

Indra's father, Dr. Srinivasaraghavan-Jones, took another sheet of cookies out of the oven. "It's called hyperhidrosis. It's very common. The eccrine sweat glands are highly concentrated in the hands. In a dry climate like Colorado's, it may even be somewhat beneficial."

"See? I've evolved into a superhuman."

"With sweaty mutant hands."

Arlo realized Indra's father might be able to help him. "Dr. S, if you needed to figure out if someone was human or not, how could you tell?"

Dr. Srinivasaraghavan-Jones took Arlo's question seriously, standing motionless with the spatula for at least ten seconds. Then he spoke. "I suppose I'd check their reflexes. It's extremely difficult to control automatic responses. For example, how someone reacts when startled."

While most signs pointed to Jaycee's strange behavior stemming from teenage love, Arlo wanted to be certain. So that evening, he crouched in the hallway outside Jaycee's door, careful not to squeak the floorboards. He leaned against the wall, tucked into the shadows. Every breath was silent. He checked his watch: 6:27. Just three minutes until dinner. At any moment, his mom would call them down to set the table.

But six thirty passed without notice. Arlo decided to keep waiting.

By six forty-five, his legs were aching. Vibrating. He wondered how lions managed to do this, quietly stalking their prey for hours on the savannah. He was about to give up on the whole thing when he finally heard his mom's voice yelling up from downstairs. "Arlo! Jaycee! Dinner!"

He listened as Jaycee's footsteps stomped behind the door. Getting closer. Closer.

The doorknob turned. Arlo waited.

The door opened a crack. Arlo waited.

Jaycee stepped through the door. Arlo pounced with a loud roar.

His sister screamed in terror, quickly transitioning to rage. "You little creep!" She pushed him back. "I'm going to murder you! So immature."

She clomped off, heading downstairs.

Arlo lay on the floor, relieved to see his sister was not hexed, mind-controlled, or a secret doppelgänger. She wanted him dead for all the normal sisterly reasons.

As he reached the bottom of the stairs, Arlo expected to see Jaycee complaining to their mother about his juvenile prank. But instead he found a stranger in the dining room. He wore jeans and heavy work boots. The back of his jacket read *Pine Mountain Garage* and featured a cartoon truck with giant tires.

Jaycee was staring at this man with the same petrifying gaze she had leveled at Uncle Wade when he'd said there was no internet. When she looked to Arlo, the man turned to face him.

"You must be Arlo. I'm Mitch. I'm a friend of your mom's."

Mitch looked like Superman's biker cousin. He was taller than Arlo's dad, but also bigger, both in the shoulders and the gut. While he didn't have a beard, it looked like one was struggling to grow out of his face. He had a bandana tied around his left wrist.

Arlo's mom came through the kitchen door, carrying green beans and potatoes. "I invited Mitch to have a home-cooked meal."

"Your mom always had the best meatloaf," Mitch said to Arlo and Jaycee.

"That wasn't my meatloaf," said their mom. "That was my mother's. Frozen onions and two cans of stewed tomatoes. This is from a magazine."

"Well, it smells like it's from heaven." He took a seat at the center of the table, the same spot Benjy had used a week earlier.

As they took their seats, Arlo and Jaycee exchanged a bewildered look. Why was this guy here? Why had their mom invited him?

Uncle Wade arrived just as food was being passed around. He had a talent for showing up after all the dinner chores were finished. He nodded in their guest's direction. "Mitch."

"Hey, Wade." Mitch helped himself to the potatoes. "Heard you got a big order. Congratulations."

Uncle Wade didn't look up from his plate. "I don't like people talking about my business."

Mitch nodded, fair enough. "So, Arlo. Your mom's told me a lot about you. I hear you're in Rangers."

"Yeah."

"Me too. I was in your company back in the day."

"How far did you get?"

"I quit after Owl. Got too busy with baseball. I was playing on a travel team and kept missing the meetings. But man, I loved the campouts. Nothing better than being out under the sky with your best friends."

"Were you in Red Patrol?"

"I was! Good guess." It wasn't that much of a guess. Jocks were always in Red Patrol. "Had to be one of four colors, right?"

"There are only three colors: red, green and blue. Senior Patrol doesn't wear neckerchiefs."

Mitch was about to say something, then he paused. He exchanged a quick look with Wade. It all happened too fast for Arlo to register what it was about.

"My mistake," said Mitch. "It was a long time ago."

Arlo didn't ask any more questions for the rest of the dinner, at least not out loud. But plenty of questions were circling in his head.

Were Uncle Wade and Mitch in Rangers together? They were about the same age. Arlo could have asked right at the table, but that risked Uncle Wade starting another tirade about something he disliked.

Why did Uncle Wade and Mitch look at each other? They didn't appear to like each other, but for that one moment, they seemed to share a common purpose.

What if there was a fourth patrol color? Not now, but back when Mitch and Uncle Wade were in Rangers. Arlo thought back to his first Rangers meeting. That night, he'd worn Wade's uniform, and shoved the neckerchief in his pocket. What color was it? Yellow?

He hadn't seen it since the night of the meeting. Had Wade taken it back?

Dessert was apple crumble with ice cream. Arlo finished his quickly and excused himself. Making sure no one was watching, he opened the door to the basement very carefully so the hinges didn't squeal. He flicked the light switch. The single bulb at the bottom of the stairs began to glow.

The chest where Uncle Wade had stored the uniform was buried under a few other boxes, but Arlo was able to dig it out. It was still unlocked from weeks earlier. Inside, he found the same memorabilia as the first time: pennants and notebooks, geodes and novelty foam can cozies.

But there was no neckerchief.

At the bottom of the chest, he discovered a small leather case. It was heavy for its size, with a snap to keep it shut and a belt loop in back like a gun holster. The leather was old and brittle, particularly around the metal bits, so he opened it gently, trying not to damage it.

Inside was a device the size of a deck of cards, but slightly rounder. It was tarnished brass, cold in his hand. He had never seen one before, but he knew immediately what it was.

A Ranger's compass.

Indra and Wu had shown him their compasses. Theirs were new, made of plastic, with dials that glowed in the dark. This was much older. Arlo flipped open the lid, revealing a tapered needle bobbing beneath the glass. As he turned around, the needle kept pointing in a single direction. North, he presumed.

Just then, he heard hinges squeal. Arlo looked back to see

Uncle Wade at the top of the stairs. Neither of them said anything as Wade slowly walked down the steps. He had to duck under the lightbulb.

Finally, he spoke. "I don't recall inviting you to go through my things."

"Sorry."

Wade pointed at the compass. "You know what that is?"

"A Ranger's compass."

"My Ranger's compass, to be specific."

"Sorry," Arlo said again.

"You know how it works?"

Arlo held it out, trying to demonstrate. "I know you set the dial for what direction you want to head. And then it's supposed to vibrate when the arrow lines up for north. But I don't see where the batteries go."

"No batteries. It's all mechanical. You gotta use the key to wind it."

Wade picked up the leather case, retrieving a tiny brass key from a pocket under the flap. Arlo never would have found it.

Wade took the compass and showed Arlo the tiny hole in back. "Gotta be careful water doesn't get in there, or the whole thing could rust and it's useless." He put the key in and twisted. "Always clockwise. Never more than twelve turns."

He flipped it back over and tested it, turning left and

right. He nodded, satisfied. But there was something else in his expression, too. A softness Arlo had never seen before, like he was remembering something—not entirely happy but not entirely sad.

Then the moment passed. Wade slid the compass into the case.

"I need a compass for Rangers," said Arlo. "For my Squirrel rank."

Wade tucked the key into its special pocket.

"I didn't want to ask mom for one, because they're pretty expensive."

Wade snapped the case shut.

"So could I use yours? I'll take good care of it, I promise."

After a long pause, Uncle Wade frowned. "Lots of people, they confuse the tool with the use of that tool. A hammer can't build a house. It can only pound a nail. Likewise, a compass can only tell you which way north is. Not which way to go."

He handed Arlo the compass.

"Best you don't forget that, or you'll get very, very lost."

20
THE COMPASS

ON SATURDAY MORNING, Arlo found a note next to the cereal box. It was from his mom. She was working a double shift at the diner and wouldn't be back until almost dinner.

An hour later, Jaycee tromped down the stairs and announced she was going out with friends. Arlo saw a dirty Toyota pick her up at the end of the driveway. Benjy was alone at the wheel.

Arlo didn't know the specific rules of learner's permits in Colorado, but he was pretty sure Benjy wasn't allowed to drive with another teenager in the car. It wasn't safe, and his mom certainly wouldn't approve. He considered calling her, or finding Uncle Wade out in his workshop. But he was only supposed to call the diner in the event of a true emergency, and this didn't seem to qualify. And short of a fire, Arlo couldn't imagine any reason he'd risk disturbing Wade. So he decided to say nothing.

Besides, this gave Arlo the whole day to work on mastering the Ranger's compass.

In order to earn his Squirrel rank, Arlo would need to complete the Dark Walk—the blindfolded test of compass proficiency. Wu had given him some basic instructions. You started by aligning the outline of the arrow with the magnetic pointer inside. That meant you were facing north. Each time the pointer crossed into the lines of the arrow, the compass would vibrate, so you could tell north without having to look down at it.

With Wu's modern battery-powered compass, the vibration was strong enough that you could feel it through your gloves. But Uncle Wade's antique compass worked differently. For starters, there was always a tiny hum from the clockwork gears inside. When the needle crossed into the arrow, the vibration was almost imperceptible, like a tiny down feather landing on your palm.

Even with his gloves off, Arlo could barely feel it. He nearly gave up in frustration.

Then he thought of the scenes in movies where the hero had to keep trying and failing hundreds of times until they finally got it. It didn't matter what the "it" was—karate, dancing, light sabers—the sequence was the same. Usually there was a cranky teacher pointing out the hero's faults, and a song playing in the background.

Arlo didn't have either of these things, but he did have all day with nothing better to do.

So to practice, Arlo would close his eyes, spin around and try to feel north. Once he'd made his decision, he would open his eyes and check whether the arrow lined up with the pointer.

The first twenty times, he was wrong.

The next twenty times, he was also wrong. Plus he was getting dizzy. He decided to alternate spinning left and spinning right.

The following twenty times, he was still wrong. But one attempt was actually pretty close. He decided to give it one more run of twenty.

On the second attempt, he got it right. Then he missed four in a row. Then he got two correct back-to-back. He started to worry that he was cheating somehow, that the sunlight coming through his eyelids was giving him an unfair advantage. (He had read how some insects navigate by checking the angle of the light, which is why moths flutter endlessly around porch lights.) So to avoid any chance of insectoid interference, he fetched his Ranger neckerchief and tied it around his face like a blindfold.

After another twenty attempts in complete darkness, he was getting it right more than half the time. More importantly, he was starting to understand why he was sometimes wrong. The compass didn't just vibrate at north. It also responded at two other points in the circle. These were slightly fainter buzzes, like echoes. When he really focused, he could tell the difference between northerly vibrations and the other ones.

Finally, he got ten right in a row. Declaring victory, he went inside and made himself a peanut butter, potato chip and jelly sandwich to celebrate.

Finding north was only step one. In order to complete the Dark Walk, he would need to be able to follow a specific path while blindfolded.

"The tricky thing is keeping your paces even," Wu had said in his initial instructions. "Once you start thinking about them, they always get longer or shorter. So you have to be able to count your steps without really being aware of them. It's harder than you'd think."

Arlo started by kicking a line in the snow with his heel. Then he started walking—pacing—ten steps up the driveway. He turned around and walked back. Perhaps because of the slope, he made it to the line in only nine steps.

So he tried again. And again. Sometimes, ten paces took him too far. Other times, not far enough.

The key, he discovered, was not looking at your feet, but focusing on the angle of your legs. Arlo imagined them as a pair of scissors, making sure he was opening them the same amount each time.

After he had reached the starting line on exactly ten paces a few times in a row, he tried again blindfolded. In some ways, this was easier, because there was nothing else to focus on but the angle of his legs. He got it right the first try, his left heel landing exactly on the starting line.

He took another break. This time he had a can of soda with his peanut butter sandwich. It was almost three o'clock. He'd spent nearly five hours pacing around the same stretch of driveway.

Now it was time to put all the skills together.

He started with the triangle, which Wu said was the easiest. In order to complete it, he would need to make two sharp turns and then end up at exactly the place he'd started.

After first lining up the compass arrow with the pointer, Arlo pulled the blindfold down over his eyes. Then he started walking ten paces forward. He quickly left the flat section of driveway, trudging through snow up over his knees. Despite the shifting terrain, he felt he was doing a good job keeping his paces.

Now for the tricky part: the turn. In order to make a triangle, he needed to pivot 120 degrees. To do that, he held the compass in his palm and started twisting the dial. With each tiny movement, it clicked. Wu said he had to go twelve clicks to the right. He counted carefully, holding his breath. He felt like a safecracker trying to break into an invisible vault.

Once he was pretty sure he had gone twelve clicks, he started to slowly turn his body, feeling the compass for the tiny vibration indicating north. That was the trick—north was always north, so once you lined it up again, you knew you were facing the right direction.

It took almost a minute before Arlo sensed he had aligned the compass. He took another ten paces forward. He was relieved when he felt the packed snow of the driveway—at least he was headed in the right direction. He accidentally started to take an eleventh step, but caught himself in time.

Once again, he twisted the dial twelve clicks to the right, then tried to find north. But something was different this time.

North wasn't where it was supposed to be.

Thinking maybe he had spun in the wrong direction, Arlo slowly turned in a full circle. He kept waiting to feel the tiny vibration.

Then the compass started humming. He could feel it quiver in his hand like an electric toothbrush, much stronger than ever before.

This didn't feel like north. This was something altogether new.

He nearly took off the blindfold but decided to keep trying. He turned a little to the left, a little to the right. The source of the hum was definitely a single direction. Arlo tried to picture which way he was facing. Given where he started, he was most likely pointing away from the house, towards the road.

Then he heard a dog barking. It was frantic. Ferocious.

Arlo pulled down the blindfold, squinting in the light. He was indeed facing the road. Cooper was barking at the forest, which wasn't so unusual. *Except,* Arlo realized, *I shouldn't be able to hear him.* The ghostly dog's bark was loud and clear in the cold air.

Closing the compass, Arlo took a few steps forward. The dog glanced back at him, then continued barking at the forest. Its tail was down. A ridge of fur stood up along its spine.

"What is it?" Arlo asked.

The dog couldn't answer. It didn't need to.

Something was coming out of the woods—a dark shape moving quickly through the trees. Arlo recognized it by its gait, even before it reached the sunlight.

It was a massive black horse.

But not an ordinary horse. Ordinary horses don't have horns like a ram, or glowing red eyes, or flames curling out of their nostrils. This horse had all of those things, and it was charging directly at him.

Arlo knew he needed to run, but his feet didn't respond. He was frozen with fear. He could only stare.

He could hear its hoofbeats in the snow.

Its mouth opened, revealing double rows of sharp teeth. Then its mouth opened even further, splitting a seam along its jaw, two petals of razory flesh. Arlo wondered if it could swallow him whole.

The horse was nearly upon him when it suddenly fell, crashing sideways into the snow. Cooper had pounced on it, ripping at its throat. The two mystical beasts were fighting savagely, snapping and scraping at each other. Arlo wanted to watch, but he knew he had to run.

His feet finally agreed.

He sprinted for the front door, slipping a few times along the way. He had just reached the porch when he heard a sickening yelp and knew that Cooper had lost the fight.

Arlo fumbled with the front door, but he finally got it open. He stepped through and slammed it behind him. He turned the lock and backed away.

Two seconds later, a massive weight slammed into the door. The hinges strained, but held. It slammed again. And again. The beast was using its horns as a battering ram, but not making any progress.

Then the banging stopped. Arlo could hear hooves clattering on the wooden porch. He wasn't sure what the horse could be doing. Pacing, maybe? Arlo started slowly backing up the staircase.

Suddenly, the door blew open, ripping off its hinges. The horse had kicked it with its hind legs like a mule.

The beast twisted back around, spotting its prey.

Arlo scrambled up the stairs, heading for his room. He could hear the horse following him, but it was having trouble. It was too big for the staircase. Each step was a struggle for the creature, its hooves sliding across the treads.

Shutting the door to his room, Arlo pushed in the little button on the doorknob to lock it. He knew the latch was nearly pointless, designed to keep someone from accidentally walking in rather than fend off a determined supernatural beast. *Jaycee's room has a proper lock, one that could actually . . .*

The clattering on the stairs had stopped. The horse had reached the upstairs hallway. Arlo could hear its hooves, muffled by the carpet. *Pum pum pum pum.* Its fur scraped against the walls as it walked. Glass broke. Arlo assumed it was a light fixture knocked off the ceiling.

Then the hooves stopped. The creature was right outside the door. Arlo could hear it breathing. And he could smell it, too: fireworks and rotten eggs.

It seemed to know Arlo was inside. Maybe it could smell him, too.

Arlo turned to the window. It was frozen shut. He banged on the frame with the heel of his hand, trying to loosen it.

The horse slammed against the door. The impact wasn't nearly as loud or as strong as it had been downstairs. *It can't ram the door,* Arlo realized. *It doesn't even have room to turn around.* The best the horse could do was smack the door with the sides of its horns. Arlo had some time.

He finally got the window open, shoving the sash all the way up. The blast of cold air invigorated him. He had been sweating in his parka.

The horse gave up banging on the door. But it was still there. Arlo could hear it moving and breathing. The beast was trying to make another plan. But what could it really do? It couldn't turn around, and even backing down the hallway would be difficult.

Then Arlo noticed light spilling under the door.

It began as a faint glow, but steadily grew brighter, as if a dimmer switch were slowly being turned up. Then a shaft of white light blasted through the old, unused keyhole. More light seeped around the edges of the door.

Whatever was happening in the hallway, it was much brighter than the sun outside.

Arlo retrieved his escape rope from the bottom drawer. As

he tied it to the radiator—using two half hitches—he saw the shadows on the wall start to move. They slowly climbed the wallpaper to the ceiling, where they began to pool together. Arlo watched as the inky darkness rippled like an upside-down puddle. This was not good.

Checking that his knot was tight, he tossed the coil of rope out the window. He had just started to climb out when suddenly—

The horse descended headfirst from the darkness above, crashing down on Arlo's bed. Its coat was glossy and wet. Spotting the boy, its mouth flared open, exposing a hundred jagged teeth.

Arlo half jumped, half fell out of the window. Grabbing the rope tight, he caught his weight but nearly pulled his arms out of their sockets. His face smashed against the side of the house. His legs flailed, trying to find the rope.

He looked up. The beast reached its head out of the window with a guttural scream. It craned its long neck, snapping at him.

Panicked, Arlo let go of the rope and fell.

The prickly bush underneath his window broke his fall. Covered in snow, it crumpled down to absorb the impact. His parka protected him from the thorns.

Lying on his back, Arlo blinked, surprised to find himself unhurt. He stared up at his window, where the beast was still futilely reaching at him. It howled in frustration. It was far too large to fit through the opening.

Arlo struggled to get to his feet. He looked back up to the window. The horse was no longer there—but a bright light was beginning to glow.

Arlo knew he needed to go. But where?

He could run down the road, but the nearest house was half a mile away, and the horse was faster.

The forest was closer. Maybe he could climb a tree. But the snow was deep; it would slow him down. And the woods were where the beast came from.

Arlo's best bet was to hide in the house, maybe the basement. Unless—

The workshop. Arlo hadn't seen his uncle all day, but he hadn't seen him leave, either. His truck was still parked in the driveway, with snow on the windshield. He was probably out there working on the big order for Jackson Hole.

But what if he wasn't? To get to the workshop, Arlo would have to run all the way around the house. If he got there and it was locked, he would have no place to hide.

He looked up at the window again. The light was gone. The beast was no longer trapped in his room. Where was it? Arlo couldn't begin to understand its shadow magic. But he was certain it was somewhere. And it was coming. Arlo had to make a choice.

He chose the workshop.

He ran. Nearing the driveway, he tripped. It surprised him more than it hurt. He picked himself up and kept running.

Turning the corner, he saw what he feared most: the workshop door was shut. Padlocked.

He stopped in his tracks, looking for another option. The laundry room door was usually kept locked because the latch didn't work right. The woodpile offered him no real protection. And even if he got to Uncle Wade's truck, he didn't have keys to drive it.

Then he heard a splintering crash coming from the second story of the house. His eyes went up to the unfinished section, where he saw movement under the blue tarps.

Suddenly, the beast leaped through the plastic. Arlo saw it all in slow motion, the horse falling through the air. It landed in a gallop, cutting a wide circle to head straight at him.

With no better option, Arlo kept running for the workshop. As he got closer, he saw the padlock was actually open, dangling from the hasp. *It was unlocked after all.* Even if Uncle Wade wasn't there, he could get inside.

Arlo yanked on the door, trying to slide it open. It was much, much heavier than he expected, moving only a few inches at a time. But that's all he needed. He squeezed through the gap and started rolling the door shut.

The gap grew narrower and narrower. He could hear the beast's hooves. It was screaming in fury.

The door shut with a satisfying thud. Arlo had made it inside.

He stepped back, catching his breath.

As his eyes adjusted to the darkness, Arlo Finch wondered if he had been better off outside.

21
THE WORKSHOP

NAMES ARE FUNNY THINGS. They can evoke an idea about the nature of an object that may have no relation to the item itself.

For example, Arlo's first bicycle was a Zephyr Fireball Maxx. He had picked it out at the store with his father, and insisted on keeping it in his room rather than the garage. The bike was sleek and fast, built for speed. That summer, he spent every afternoon racing down the dead-end street near their house in Philadelphia. He imagined himself winning the Tour de France on it one day.

It wasn't until he went back to school in September that he saw an identical bike locked next to his on the rack. It had the same tires, same frame, same everything. Except it had a different name: the Mountaineer. This was a slow but sturdy trail bike, designed for rocky paths and steep slopes.

Yet it was the exact same bike. Only the name had changed.

Uncle Wade had called the building out back his "workshop." The name had made Arlo think of Santa's workshop, or the show on public television where the man with suspenders made drawers with dovetail joints. In his mind, Arlo had pictured his uncle working at long tables with various taxidermy animals in different stages of assembly: a half-stuffed eagle over here, a rabbit being glued over there. He imagined the workshop to be cluttered but comfortable, perhaps even cozy, much like the house.

This was incorrect, a misconception based on the term *workshop*.

If Arlo had named this place, he would have called it "the scary dark terror shed." Because that would have been accurate.

To his left, a wall held rusty blades of every conceivable shape and length. Some looked like they had been taken from various machines: shredders, plows, lawn mowers. Others seemed to have no purpose other than being terrifying. The blades hung from hooks in neat lines stretching up to the ceiling, where more pieces dangled from wires overhead.

To his right, a lopsided cabinet held hundreds of disassembled dolls. They seemed to be sorted into categories—heads, legs, torsos, arms—but the individual pieces were packed randomly on overflowing shelves. Dirty doll faces stared at Arlo with unblinking eyes.

Straight ahead, he could see dim light coming through dirty plastic sheeting draped from the ceiling. It seemed to serve as an entrance to the back of the shed.

Everything about this space was so unsettling that he almost forgot about the monster trying to kill him. Almost.

"Uncle Wade!? Are you out here?" Arlo could see his breath in the narrow crack of light spilling through the door.

There was no answer.

If his uncle was here, he was on the other side of the plastic sheeting. Psyching himself up, Arlo carefully pushed it aside, revealing a larger room beyond. A wave of warm air hit his face.

His uncle was sitting on a stool with his back to him, giant headphones over his ears. He was busy working on something, picking up and setting down tools and brushes. A curl of smoke rose from a soldering iron. An electric heater glowed at his feet.

"Uncle Wade?"

Still no answer. Arlo could hear the music spilling out of

the headphones: loud heavy metal, all thrashing drums and distorted guitars.

But there was another sound, too, one that reminded Arlo of the wooden xylophone from third-grade music class. His gaze drifted up to the rafters, where five dark wooden boards with Chinese writing hung from wires. A circular hammer swung wildly in the middle, striking the boards, each of which played a different note. It was like a wind chime. Except there was no wind. Arlo had no idea what was making the hammer swing so erratically.

"Uncle Wade!" This time he really shouted. Still no answer. The music in his uncle's headphones was simply too loud. Seeing no other option, Arlo finally tapped him on the arm.

Uncle Wade was so startled he fell off his stool, crashing into a series of cardboard boxes. He finally landed on his back next to a stuffed beaver holding a toothbrush.

"Sorry!" Arlo offered his hand to help him up. Uncle Wade refused it, pushing himself to his knees.

"You know you're not supposed to come out here. That's the one rule."

"I know, but . . ."

"No buts, no exceptions." Wade stood up, untangling himself from the headphone cord. "This is my sanctuary. This is where I do my art!"

"I know! It's just . . ."

With a *tsh-tsh*, Wade shushed him, listening. He looked up to the wooden boards dangling above them, suddenly concerned. "How long has it been doing that?"

"I don't know," said Arlo. "What is it?"

"It's an alarm. Something's here that shouldn't be." He pushed past Arlo, headed for the front room.

"I know! That's why—"

Wade was already through the plastic sheeting. Arlo didn't want to follow him. But he didn't want to be alone, either. He caught up to his uncle just as he was starting to slide the heavy door open.

"No, no! Don't! It's out there!" Arlo blocked the handle, trying to stop him. "It's a monster. It came out of the woods." His uncle relented, listening as Arlo continued. "I was out front, practicing with the compass. Your compass. And then it started to vibrate."

"That's what it's supposed to do. That's north."

"It wasn't north. It was something else. And then this thing—like a horse, but not a horse—came charging out of the forest. Cooper tried to stop it, but—" Arlo suddenly realized he hadn't heard the dog's bark since the first encounter. "I think it killed him."

"Cooper's already dead. You know that. He's a ghost dog."

"But he was fighting the monster. I saw it."

Uncle Wade's eyebrows scrunched together, his expression skeptical but not dismissive. He nodded. "All right. Let's take a look." Grabbing a shovel as a weapon, he slid the door open before Arlo could stop him.

Wade squinted in the crack of sunlight. Cold air spilled around the edges of the door. Arlo braced for impact.

But it never came.

"There's nothing out there." Wade pushed the door open wider so Arlo could see.

Uncle Wade was clearly going blind, because the horse was no more than twenty feet away, pacing back and forth like a lion at the zoo.

"You really don't see it? It's right there." Arlo pointed.

Wade shrugged. "I don't see anything. But that doesn't mean it's not there. Lots of eldritch things are basically invisible. That's why you don't see photos of them."

"Then why can I see it?"

"Same reason you see Cooper, I guess. Maybe it's your weird eyes." Arlo knew he didn't mean it as an insult. "What's it doing?"

"It's just walking around. Why isn't it trying to get in?"

"I got serious wards on this building. Not just the alarm, but real totems built into the walls. Cost me a pretty penny. But it keeps the bad stuff out."

"So we're safe? We can just stay here and wait for it to go away?"

Wade shook his head. "Waiting's no good. What happens when your mom comes back? Or your sister? Just because they can't see it doesn't mean it's not there. We're gonna have to find a way to deal with it."

"You mean, kill it?"

Wade scoffed. "Good luck with that." He headed back through the plastic doorway. Arlo followed him, nervous to leave the shed door open.

He found his uncle rooting through a particularly deep pile of junk on one of the side tables, searching for something. He didn't seem as panicked as Arlo thought he should be. "Best we can hope for is to abjure it. Send it back where it belongs."

"You know how to do that?"

"Not precisely." He pulled out a book. Wrong one. He tossed it aside.

"But in general?"

"General theory, sure. First we gotta know what we're dealing with." He finally found what he was looking for. It was an old book, warped with water damage. Arlo instantly recognized the cover: *Culman's Bestiary*. Uncle Wade had had one all this time. "Now, you said it's a horse?"

"Like a horse. But with horns."

Wade skimmed through the index in the back of the book. "What kind of horns? Elk? Rhino? Unicorn?"

"There are unicorns?"

"What, you think people are just making them up?"

"I don't know. I mean, what else is real? Dragons? Giants?"

Uncle Wade snapped his reading glasses together. They connected with magnets at the bridge of his nose. "Let's focus on the thing trying to kill you, all right?"

"It had round horns. They curled back on themselves." Arlo traced the air with his fingers. "And its mouth opened super, super wide."

"Sounds like a nightmare," said Wade, flipping through the book.

Arlo nodded. "It was."

"No, I mean a Night Mare. Two words. 'Mare' is another name for a horse."

Arlo nodded. Night Mare was the perfect name for the creature.

Wade had a hard time finding the page he was looking for. Then he realized several of the pages were stuck together. He carefully peeled them apart, ripping the paper in a few places. He turned the book to show Arlo the illustration. "Is that it?"

It was just a pen-and-ink drawing, but it was definitely the same creature. "That's it. That's what's out there."

Wade read the entry to himself in a whispered mumble. Arlo didn't catch much of it. His attention drifted over to the workbench, where he could see what his uncle was working on. It wasn't like any of the standard taxidermy animals in the dining room. This was much more elaborate, featuring a badger with a crown slumped back in a throne made of doll arms. Three squirrels dressed as jesters were juggling for the Badger King's amusement while a pigeon with a sword kept watch. Even in its unfinished state, the piece was extraordinary, equal parts creepy and beautiful and funny.

Arlo pointed to it. "That's really cool."

"Oh. Thank you. Trying something new." Then, back to the book—"We need to find some salt."

According to *Culman's Bestiary*, shadow creatures like Night Mares could only cross into our world through moonlit lakes deep in the Long Woods. The magical water from those pools clung to their fur, protecting them while they traveled. *That's why it looked so glossy,* thought Arlo.

Wade read aloud from the book. "Once the water dries, or is tainted by salt, the creature is immediately dispelled."

"So we just have to dump salt on it."

"Exactly."

"Do you have any salt?"

"Not out here. Only salt you're gonna find is in the house. There's some in the kitchen by the stove."

But that meant leaving the safety of the scary dark terror shed. Arlo waited for his uncle to volunteer to make the run. Neither spoke for a few moments. Then Wade nodded.

"Way I see it, you're better qualified to do this," he said.

"You can see it. I can't. Plus you're smaller and can run faster."

"I can't run faster than a horse."

"True. That's definitely true." But Wade seemed to be forming a plan. "Let's see if we can get you a head start."

Before Arlo could respond, Wade ripped the plastic sheeting down. Arlo could now see directly out the open door, where the horse was still pacing, waiting for them to come out.

But his uncle couldn't see it. "It's still there, right?"

Arlo nodded.

"Then let's send you out the back." Wade pulled a table away from the wall, sliding boxes to reveal the wood behind. He plugged a circular saw into a heavy orange extension cord. It whirred as the blade spun.

"You're going to cut a hole?"

"A little one. You're pretty small." He knelt down to start cutting.

"Won't that mess up the wards? The ones protecting us?"

"Huh. Maybe. Never was quite clear on how these mystical things work. Suppose you could run out the front—"

Arlo cut him off. "It's okay. You can do it."

He watched as his uncle sawed through the wall. If the wards had fallen, the horse didn't seem to know it. The beast was still pacing back and forth on the snowy driveway.

With two more cuts, Wade had made an opening the size of a doggie door. On the far side, the snow was deep and crusty, but sunlight was peeking through the top few inches. "This ought to work. Now, you're going to want to run around to the back patio door because—"

"The laundry room door is locked."

"Exactly. I know for a fact the sliding glass door is unlocked because I went out there this morning." Uncle Wade never locked the house, only his workshop. "Once you're inside, don't stop until you've got the sodium chloride in hand. That's the scientific name for salt."

"How do I use it?"

"Book doesn't say, but I suspect you can just throw it on the horse. You'll know if it works, because if it doesn't, you'll be dead."

There was no faulting Uncle Wade's logic, but Arlo wished he could be a little gentler in how he said things.

Arlo got on his belly, preparing to squeeze through the hole. Worried that his parka would get caught, he took it off. Freezing was the least of his worries.

"Think like a squirrel," said Wade. "They just get that nut and go."

Squirrel, Arlo thought as he exhaled. *Be a brave squirrel.*

"You want me to give you a shove?" asked Wade. Arlo nodded. That might help. "Okay. Three, two, one."

Uncle Wade pushed. Arlo dug with his arms, swimming through the snow. In just three seconds, he was outside in the blinding sunlight. He scrambled to his feet and ran as fast as he could.

He didn't look back. He didn't have to. The horse shrieked as it spotted him.

Racing along the back of the house, Arlo passed the laundry room. The patio was in sight. He nearly slipped as he reached the sliding glass door. He yanked the handle.

It didn't budge. Locked. *Jaycee*, he thought. She hated when Wade left things unlocked. ("Any rando could just walk in.") She must have locked it before she went off with Benjy.

The beast was charging straight for him. He had no choice but to run. He cut hard around the corner of the house, knowing the horse would have to circle. He could hear the hoofbeats. It was close.

Rounding the next corner, he was at the front of the house. The porch was just ahead. Out of the corner of his eye, he could see the horse gaining on him. Arlo raced up the steps, through the busted-down front door.

Hooves on wood. Another shriek. Arlo could feel the creature's breath. It was right behind him.

He cut right, dashing through the dining room for the kitchen door. The horse was slower inside. Clumsy. Its size worked against it.

Arlo made it into the kitchen. He knew what he was looking for: a blue paper canister with a metal tab. Wade had said the salt was by the stove. But there was nothing like that there.

He whirled around, checking the countertops. Just then, the horse crashed through the swinging door. Arlo backed away. There was still the bathroom. Maybe he could squeeze out through the window.

Then he saw it: the salt shaker. It was on the kitchen table, next to the pepper. It wasn't the canister he'd been searching for, but at least it was salt. It might be enough.

Unfortunately, there was a monster in his way. The giant creature was squeezing through the door.

What would a squirrel do? Arlo thought. They were always facing bigger predators. Most times, they ran away. But what did they do when they were cornered?

They used their size to their advantage.

The horse was now all the way in the kitchen. As its

mouth flared open to bite, Arlo saw his chance. He dove between its legs, scampering underneath the kitchen table. Its rear hooves nearly smashed his hand.

The beast reared around, crashing into the chairs. The table shook. Arlo saw the pepper shaker fall and smash open on the floor. But the salt shaker was still up there.

Reaching blindly, Arlo searched the tabletop. He passed over the napkins and the sugar bowl. The table shook again as the horse turned. Suddenly, Arlo felt it: a glass rectangle with a metal top. He grabbed it and pulled it down.

The salt shaker. Arlo smiled with relief.

The monster leaned down on its haunches, trying to get to its prey. Slime dripped from its jagged teeth.

Arlo scrambled back for the door, heading into the dining room. He sprinted out the front, twisting the cap off the salt shaker.

He jumped the front steps, racing across the snow. Uncle Wade was standing in the driveway, carrying the shovel like a club. "Did you get it?!"

"I got it!" Arlo stopped and spun around to look back at the house. The horse was charging out the front door, leaping from the porch.

Arlo poured the salt into his hand and dropped the shaker. He had to wait until the beast was close enough. Too soon and the salt wouldn't hit it.

The monster lowered its horns as it charged. It was going to ram him.

Arlo felt his heart in his throat. Some of the salt was slipping between his fingers. Did he even have enough?

The horse was forty feet away. Thirty.

Arlo stood his ground, defiant.

Twenty feet. Ten.

Arlo threw the salt. It fanned in the air like playground sand.

The creature leaped. It looked like a fist trying to smash him.

Arlo didn't flinch.

The beast hit the salt spray and exploded in a thunderclap of smoke. After the boom came a pop and a crackle. For a few moments, the inky vapors hung in the air, still holding the shape of a horse. Then they settled, falling as black ash on the white snow.

The beast had been dispelled.

His ears still ringing, Arlo looked over to his uncle.

"Heck yeah, I saw it," shouted Wade. "Flash! Boom! That was awesome."

— 22 —
REPAIRS

UNCLE WADE LEANED ON HIS SHOVEL. "We should probably try to get stuff cleaned up before your mom and sister get back."

Arlo agreed.

The biggest concern was the front door, which lay flat in the entry, ripped from its hinges. His uncle used a tube of epoxy to glue the frame back together. It smelled like melting plastic and vinegar potato chips. Arlo helped him hoist the door back into place, tapping the pins in with a hammer.

While his uncle worked on reattaching the lock, Arlo traced the beast's path through the house.

Each step had left a hoofprint of cinders and ash. The wooden steps were easily swept, but the shag carpet upstairs required the ancient vacuum cleaner. He ran it back and forth, never sure if it was actually picking the soot up or just grinding it in. Either way, the carpet eventually returned to an even color.

The kitchen was easily tidied. To repair the pepper shaker, Wade provided a different glue, one he assured Arlo wasn't poisonous. You had to really look to see the crack.

The hallway light fixture was hopelessly broken, however. They swapped it out for one in the linen closet. It didn't look anything like the original, but Wade said that didn't matter. "No one goes around looking for what's different. They're too wrapped up in their own business."

Arlo soon learned he was right. When Jaycee got home, she went straight to her room without commenting on the hall light, or the dirty carpet, or the faint dents in the front door. As long as it didn't mess with her routine, the house could be on fire for all she cared.

As his uncle finished a few last tweaks on the front doorknob, Arlo spotted the headlights of his mother's car turning onto the driveway.

"What do we do if another monster shows up?" he asked.

Wade snapped his toolbox shut. "I've got a buddy who can put some wards on the house proper. But I figure you ought to keep that salt shaker handy, just in case."

Arlo's mom parked and switched off the ignition. Uncle Wade headed back to his workshop. At that moment, Arlo realized how few words he had actually heard his mother and uncle exchange. They were less like siblings and more like reluctant roommates. They stayed out of each other's way.

As his mom headed up the front path, she paused. She looked over at Arlo. "Something you want to tell me?"

What was it? What did she know?

She pointed over to Arlo's escape rope, still dangling from his window. In all the tidying up, he had forgotten to put it away.

"I was practicing my knots." That wasn't technically a lie. Those two half hitches had saved his life.

His mom shook her head, more tired than angry. "Just please be careful. That's a big drop. I don't want you getting hurt." Arlo nodded. "What else did you do today?"

He thought back, suddenly realizing how eventful the day had been even before the monster tried to kill him. "I figured out how to use the Ranger's compass. It's really hard, but I think I understand it now."

———◦●◦———

As he was closing his curtains before bed, Arlo thought he saw movement down by the road.

His first instinct was to find Uncle Wade, but then he remembered hearing the truck driving away after dinner.

Wade had presumably gone to see his friend about installing new wards on the house.

That meant if something was out there, Arlo would need to investigate it himself. He grabbed his flashlight and salt shaker—he'd discovered a spare in one of the kitchen cabinets—and slipped quietly downstairs.

He was already in his pajamas, so he put on his boots and his parka. The front door opened silently. If anything, it worked better than before.

The snow crunched under his feet. The night was much colder than the afternoon. The wind made his ears ache. He should have worn his hat.

Arlo swept the flashlight across the shadows. Nothing but trees.

He made it all the way down to the road. Whatever he'd seen was gone. Or, more likely, was all in his imagination.

Just as he turned back to the house, he saw it. A shape rushed at him, low to the ground. The light passed right through it.

It was Cooper.

The ghostly dog limped a bit as he walked, but seemed otherwise unhurt. He was as undead as ever. Arlo held out his hand, but Cooper ignored it. He was back to his normal, endless routine.

Arlo smiled. "Good boy."

23
THE BONFIRE

FOR THE NEXT FEW WEEKS, nothing attempted to kill Arlo Finch. Which was frustrating, because he was really prepared.

Over Christmas break, he had made a list of sixteen creatures in *Culman's Bestiary* that could be dispelled with the salt he always kept in his pocket. He had attached a carabiner to his escape rope, bringing his window exit time down by seven seconds. He had even started doing push-ups every night in case it came down to a hand-to-hand struggle.

Instead, his closest brush with death came from a post-holiday cold that was passed around the sixth grade like the class guinea pig on weekends. He only missed one day of school, and no exams. His fever barely broke a hundred degrees.

Arlo would never admit it, but he was growing a little disappointed in whatever forces had conspired to kill him. He could see it in his friends' faces, too. Every morning, they were happy to see him, but also a little surprised. "Nothing?" asked Wu.

"I nearly got hit by a car, but it was mostly my fault. I wasn't looking."

Indra tried to remain optimistic. "Accidents are the most common cause of death for young people. Maybe they're trying to make it look ordinary."

"It was Mrs. Mayes just now in the parking lot. If they wanted my teacher to kill me, they'd have her assign another research paper on the Fertile Crescent."

But on the third Friday in January, Arlo suspected that this might finally be the day.

It was the weekend of the Alpine Derby, the only campout of the year that spanned both Friday and Saturday nights. Since they were going straight from class to the mountains, they'd worn their uniforms to school. Indra and Wu endured endless questions from Merilee Myers about each of their patches and the significance of their pentagonal shape. "Sometimes I dream about the number five," she said. "And when I wake up, my goldfish is staring at me."

At recess, Arlo practiced his knots and compass work with Indra and Wu. After lunch, they raced to the library for one last look through *Culman's Bestiary*. Mrs. Fitzrandolph had gotten so used to them asking for it that she left the drawer unlocked provided they each promised to check out one actual book without monsters in it. (Arlo chose *My Side of the Mountain*. He had always wanted a trained falcon.)

When the bell rang at 3:05, they went straight to the church parking lot with their backpacks. An hour later, they were hiking to their campsite, digging out to set up their tents. Connor triple-checked the wards, but Arlo felt remarkably safe even without their protection.

Unlike a normal campout, this weekend there were thirty patrols from eight different companies up on the mountain. Everywhere he looked, he could see Rangers and Wardens cooking by lantern light. He saw snaplights, snowball fights and flaming marshmallows on sticks. If something wanted to attack him, there was no way it could sneak up. Plus it would have to get through a lot of innocent people first.

That was a grim thought, Arlo admitted. But comforting.

A roaring jet of flame shot fifty feet into the air, so hot that Arlo made sure his eyebrows hadn't burned off. Then the fiery column split into three glowing strands, the sections bobbing and weaving around one another to form a braid.

The three hundred assembled Rangers cheered wildly.

225

The opening-night bonfire was an Alpine Derby tradition, but tonight's entertainment was unprecedented.

Arlo watched the three Wardens standing at the edge of the fire. As they moved their hands, the flames followed, flowing like molten glass. The Warden closest to Arlo was a bearded man with suspenders. He seemed to be the leader, nodding directions to the other two.

"How are they doing that?" asked Arlo.

"They're firecraefters," said Indra. "Elemental magic. Super advanced and dangerous."

Wu leaned in. "I heard they were all Bears back when they were in Rangers. They teach them that at the secret camp." Arlo hadn't considered that many of the Wardens were likely former Rangers. He'd thought they were all just ordinary parents.

Once the braid was complete, the bearded Warden squeezed his hand into a fist. The three strands of fire fused at the top.

"All right!" he shouted. "We've done our part. Now it's your turn. Rangers, snaplights! On three." All around Arlo, Rangers raised their hands, including Wu and Indra. Arlo decided he would try as well. "One, two, three!"

Hundreds of snaplights shot from the crowd. As they rose, a strange gravity bent their path until they formed a swirling ring around the pillar. New snaplights continuously added to the shape, which kept growing brighter.

Wu launched one that made it to the pillar. So did the twins. Indra got two. Arlo kept snapping, but he couldn't get anything to happen. He tried with his left hand as well. Thinking maybe his hands were too dry, he licked his fingertips. Still nothing. No spark, no light.

"What am I doing wrong?"

"Nothing," Connor said. "It will just happen when it happens." That was easy for him to say as he snapped a dozen lights in a row.

Frustrated, Arlo put his gloves back on. He looked back at the firecraefters. The bearded man seemed to be straining, fighting to hold on to the fiery pillar like it was a vicious dog on a leash. No one else seemed to notice. They were all too busy shooting snaplights.

Arlo followed the man's gaze to the top of the column, where the flames were starting to shift. They stretched and flattened, reaching over the top of the ring. It almost looked like the head of a snake.

The bearded man was now clearly struggling. Arlo could see him sweating. The other two Wardens looked over, concerned.

Now the snaplights themselves were starting to drift, pulled from their orbit. Some went up, tracing the outline of an alligator's snout with the horns of a goat. Other lights fanned out to form glowing wings.

Arlo could see it clearly. It was—

"A dragon." He said it in unison with a girl standing beside him.

He looked to his left to find Rielle. Everyone else had vanished. The two of them were standing at the deserted bonfire, staring in awe at the massive flaming dragon suspended above them.

It didn't move. It simply burned. Yet Arlo sensed it was somehow alive.

"It's sleeping," Rielle said. "It's been sleeping for centuries."

"How did it get here?" asked Arlo.

"It made this place. This is its dream."

"Then how did *we* get here?" asked Arlo.

Rielle looked over. "We found our way. That's what makes us so valuable."

Arlo could see the fire reflected in her mismatched eyes. As he looked back to the dragon, he could feel Rielle leave. Or maybe he had left her. If this was all a dream, he was waking up.

The Wardens were back at the bonfire, fighting to control the flames. Arlo could see real panic, yet all around, the Rangers were cheering wildly. They assumed the fiery dragon was part of the show.

The bearded Warden nodded to the other two, signaling

them to hold it still. Then he clasped his hands, aiming them at the center of the flames. He flicked his fingers apart.

The dragon exploded into thousands of tiny points of light. They descended like fireflies, fading into the night.

All around him, Arlo heard the Rangers cheering. Wu was the loudest of them all. "That was awesome! I want to be a firecraefter."

"Obviously," said Indra. "You're already a pyro."

Arlo knew he needed to tell his friends about seeing Rielle. But he wanted to know something else first.

As the patrols headed back to their campsites, he found the bearded Warden talking with a group of other adults. He waited until they finished, then went up to the man as he was lighting his lantern. The Warden's hand was trembling as he held the match.

"You didn't mean to make the dragon, did you?" asked Arlo.

The bearded man looked over. His eyes narrowed, sizing Arlo up. "Fire's a tricky thing. It surprises you sometimes."

He blew out the match.

24

THE SPRINT

THEY WERE WINNING.

At the front of the sled, Arlo couldn't see how close the other patrols were. But he knew Blue was ahead.

They had taken the lead at the midpoint, swinging wide around the giant totem pole to keep their speed up. Red Patrol had gotten there first, but got stuck in the turn. Connor had predicted it when they scouted the course that morning. "By the time we get to our heat, twenty other patrols will have carved up the snow." That was no problem in the straightaways—in fact, the flattened sections were faster— but you wanted clean powder for the turn.

So Blue Patrol stayed on the outside, and let the others get jammed up in the ruts of previous runs. Arlo could hear

Russell Stokes shouting at his Red teammates while they repositioned their sled. Even Green with its jingling sleigh bells was struggling, caught behind two surprisingly strong patrols from Nederland Company.

While the others were jammed up in the bend, Blue was already headed home. All the weeks of sled practice were paying off. Mr. Henhao was performing perfectly.

Not that it was easy. Arlo's lungs burned. His legs strained. But he kept running. They were going to win. The finish line was twenty yards away. Fifteen. Ten.

Then he heard it. A whoop. A scrape. Pounding footsteps.

Russell Stokes was suddenly right beside him. Then he was passing him. Red Patrol was passing them.

Arlo was running faster than he had ever run in his life, but it wasn't enough. Russell's hand broke the toilet paper finishing-line ribbon. The back of the Red sled crossed before the front of the Blue sled.

There was no question, no debate. Red had won. Blue came in second.

The moment they crossed the line, Arlo collapsed on the snow, staring up at the bright blue sky as he caught his breath. Every nerve was twitching. He was hot and cold simultaneously. His stomach itched from where his T-shirt was rubbing.

He wiped his eyes. It was sweat, not tears. He was pretty sure.

At the corner of his vision, he saw Russell Stokes. He was leaning on his knees, catching his breath. He traded a few high fives with his buddies. Then Russell noticed Arlo watching and held his fingers in an L against his forehead. Loser.

Connor wasn't disappointed. Or at least he did a good job of pretending not to be. "Look, we came in second in our heat. We beat Green Patrol, which is amazing."

"We should have beaten Red," said Wu. "We were ahead."

"Yeah, and they were faster," said Jonas. "Look at them. They're all jocks. They run track and play football. We can practice all we want, but they're always going to be faster. There's no way we can beat them."

"You're right," said Connor. "We can't outrun them. But remember, the sprint only counts for ten points. We've still got all the stations plus spirit and sled-judging. We can still beat them."

"We'd have to be perfect," said Wu.

"Then let's be perfect. Because they won't be. Think about it: Are they better than us at knots? No. How about signaling? No way. Julie and Jonas are unmatched."

Connor was right: the twins were scarily good at signaling. It was as if they were communicating psychically.

"Wu is great at fire-building. They're not going to be able to boil water faster than us."

Arlo had seen Wu go from a single scrape of flint and steel to a roaring blaze in less than a minute. Wu always knew exactly when to add more kindling and just how hard to blow. He called it his dragon breath.

"And nobody is better than Indra at map-reading," said Connor. "Red Patrol is going to get lost at some point, I guarantee. That will cost them time."

"We could cross the finish line first," said Indra. "That alone would make up the points we lost."

"Guys, we can do this," said Connor. "Seriously. We can win." With nods and bitten lips, the patrol was coming around. He had sold them on his vision. Until—

"You forgot Arlo," said Julie. "What's he good at?"

Arlo could feel them all staring. Judging. Trying to think of something nice to say. He had been happy to be overlooked. The truth was, he wasn't particularly good at anything.

"Spirit," said Connor. "He's our mascot. He's going to win this for us."

Wu punched him in the shoulder. Arlo smiled.

"Let's practice our yell," said Connor. "It's gotta be flawless."

They lined up. Arlo was on the end because he was the shortest. Connor shouted, "One!"

The twins shouted, "Two!"

Wu and Indra shouted, "Three!"

Arlo shouted, "Four!"

Clap your hands!
Stomp your feet!
Blue Patrol just can't be beat!
Faster than a snowshoe hare,
Stronger than a grizzly bear.
Both tomorrow and today,
Blue Patrol will lead the way!

— 25 —
KNAUGHTS

THE ALPINE DERBY WAS DESIGNED to measure a patrol's competence in six fundamental outdoor skills, which went by the acronym SKRIFT: Signals, Knots, Rescue, Identification, Fire and Teamwork.

Each skill was the focus of one station along the derby course. While patrols could prepare in a general sense—such as practicing their knots and first aid—they had no way of knowing a station's specific challenge until they arrived. Only when they checked in with the station captain would they learn what they needed to do.

"Last year for Teamwork, we had to build a bridge over a ditch and get everyone across," explained Connor. "Which would have been easy except they didn't give you enough logs. The trick was that you had to wait until another patrol got there and share logs with them. Green Patrol was the first to figure that out."

To do well, patrols needed to be fast and flawless. The maximum score for each station was ten points, but time penalties and other deductions made that hard to achieve. "Last year, we got a three in Signals. We just couldn't do it. Patrols kept passing us."

While the derby was meant to measure six skills, a seventh factor played a major part: luck. Patrols were required to visit the stations in the order specified on their route card, yet some were nearly a mile apart. "If you draw a bad route card, you can end up backtracking a lot. It slows you down."

With sled-judging complete—they'd received nine out of ten points—it was time for the main event. Patrol leaders gathered at the starting line, where each chose a sealed envelope from a stack, holding it high in the air. The bearded Warden from the night before called out, "Patrol leaders! May your path be safe!"

In unison, they responded, "May your aim be true!"

"On my mark, let the forty-ninth annual Alpine Derby begin!" All the Rangers cheered, then the Warden thunderclapped. It was so loud it echoed off distant mountains.

Connor raced back to the patrol, ripping open the envelope

as he ran. He handed the route card to Indra, who started tracing a map.

"We have Rescue first, followed by Knots. They're really far apart."

Jonas shook his head. "We got a bad draw."

"Not really. Signals, Identification and Fire are next, and they're all pretty close. Teamwork's on the far side, though. It puts us a long way from the finish line."

"Then we'll run to the end," said Connor. "We'll give everything we've got."

———•◉•———

Running at a steady pace, they were the first patrol to reach Rescue. The station captain—a Senior Patrol member from another company—handed them instructions glued to a board.

An exploding aurora geyser has left everyone in your patrol temporarily blinded, except for one member who fell from a tree and broke both legs. Choose one member of your patrol to be the victim. The rest of the patrol must tend to the injuries, construct a stretcher and transport the victim to the medical tent while blindfolded. The victim can see and provide directions.

Indra squealed with delight. They had practiced almost exactly this scenario just a week earlier.

Wu was the designated victim. He called out instructions while never losing his cool. Arlo helped splint Wu's left leg before switching to stretcher construction. At no point was he confused about what he needed to do next. The patrol was moving as a single twelve-handed organism.

The path to the medical tent was filled with obstacles—mostly barrels and posts—but Wu carefully guided his team as they carried him on the stretcher. "Set me down!" he shouted. "We're here!" They heard a whistle, their signal to take off their blindfolds. Arlo squinted in the bright light, looking back over the course. They had finished before other patrols had even picked victims.

Connor collected their route card from the captain, checking the score. "Ten points!" he shouted. The patrol cheered. They were off to a perfect start.

On their way to Knots, they crossed paths with both the Red and Green Patrols. Each had apparently finished their first challenge quickly, and were now headed to the next closest station. "They got a better draw," said Jonas.

"Let's run our race, not theirs," said Connor.

Knots seemed straightforward—they simply had to tie the same ten knots they had practiced for months. The surprise was the rope itself: it was thirty feet long and six inches thick. Working as a team, they dragged it through the snow to form the necessary loops and hitches. Not only was it exhausting, it was hard to visualize how to tie each knot at such a giant scale. Arlo helped tie the bowline, acting the part of the rabbit as he crawled out of the hole and around the tree.

Once again, they got a perfect ten points. "Let's not get cocky," Connor warned.

For Signals, the instructions called for patrols to split in half, with one group hiking to a distant hilltop. Once there, they had to communicate a series of code words back and forth between locations. Arlo, Connor and Jonas were on the hillside team, while the other three stayed at base.

There was no required method of signaling. Arlo saw that most patrols were using mirrors or flashlights to do Morse code, but Jonas and Julie had been practicing flag semaphore for weeks. Originally used by ships at sea, semaphore was potentially faster. By holding flags at specific angles, the twins could send messages one letter at a time. "B-L-U-E-B-E-R-R-Y," called out Jonas, reading his sister's positions. Arlo looked up *blueberry* in the provided chart, finding the corresponding answer: *elephant.*

Within two minutes, they had gotten all of the words and were racing back down to join the others. Not only did they receive ten points, the station captain said they were the fastest patrol yet.

Indra and Connor could handle Identification by themselves—they were walking encyclopedias of naturecraeft. The rest of the patrol simply followed them as they quickly distinguished spruces from firs (pinereading), warblers from wrens (birdsighting), and squirrel prints from chipmunk (tracking). "The tail spray is a dead giveaway," said Connor.

The only debate came over a pile of droppings. Based on the color and texture, Indra was certain it was moose poop. Connor was equally convinced it was elk, given the smaller size. "Not all moose are full-grown," Indra argued. "Little moose have little butts. Just look how much cellulose there is. That's nothing like an elk." Connor was finally persuaded. He wrote "moose" on the clipboard.

But when he returned from the station captain, even Arlo could identify the look on his face. Those were elk droppings. At the one station that should have been a lock for a perfect score, Blue Patrol had only gotten nine points.

"Lots of patrols are going to get that one wrong," Connor said as they left the station. "I doubt anyone gets a perfect score." But Arlo could tell Indra was upset. Even as Wu sailed through the water-boiling section of the Fire challenge, she hung back from the group, silently cursing her overconfidence. When it came time for the patrol yell, she cheered with gusto. But the moment the station captain stopped watching, her smile faded.

Once the fire was approved, it was time to eat. Alpine Derby rules required patrols to take a full hour for lunch, so there was no reason to rush their chicken chili. Arlo ate two bowls with extra cheese and crackers. Indra barely finished her first.

Arlo wanted to tell her that everyone makes mistakes. That the patrol was lucky to have her. That they wouldn't even be here if not for her persistence. Indra stopped him before he could say a word. "It's okay. I'm just processing the emotion. One day I'm going to use this experience in my memoirs."

Arlo admitted he wasn't sure what memoirs were.

"It's when a famous person writes about their life and describes the bad stuff they went through. It's important to have enough bad stuff or it just seems like bragging, and no one likes that. So messing up today, that's really helpful, because it shows that I'm human."

Arlo wondered if trying to seem human was a sign that someone wasn't very human. But there wasn't time to discuss it further. The patrol was packing up, because in five minutes they would be released to run to their final station.

⬤

When they reached Teamwork, they found three other patrols waiting to go in. The challenge evidently took a long time, and the station had built up a backlog over the course of the day.

"We've been here half an hour," said a patrol leader from Canyon City. "And we still have two stations after this. We may just take the penalty and go out of sequence." She was being practical. It was already after one o'clock, and patrols needed to cross the finish line by five or be disqualified.

"I told you we got a bad draw," said Jonas. "If we'd had this station at the start, we wouldn't be waiting around." This time, Connor didn't try to talk Jonas out of his sulk.

After another ten minutes, the Canyon City patrol turned their sled around and left. Now there were only two teams ahead of Blue.

To pass the time, Arlo built a snowman. Jonas and Connor paced. Julie and Indra talked with a girl in another patrol. Wu fell asleep against the sled.

A second patrol decided to leave. Now there was only one ahead of Blue.

Arlo started making a snowdog for his snowman. He quickly realized why he had never seen one before—without legs, snowdogs just looked like alligators or ottomans.

The station captain waved in the next patrol, then pointed at Blue. It was their time, too. Arlo gave up on his snowdog. His gloves were wet, so he took them off.

The Teamwork challenge required patience and communication. Patrols were given four special ropes. Each had the ends fused together to form a circle with the diameter of a hula hoop. Using only these ropes, they needed to disassemble, move and reassemble a four-piece totem pole. Each time someone's hand touched the pole itself, it was a one-point deduction.

"What's the most points any patrol has lost?" asked Wu.

"Ten," said the captain. "Had a lot of patrols leave here with zero."

The trick, they quickly discovered, was to loop the ropes over each section from multiple angles, then pull against one another to lift and move it. "Like a suspension bridge," Wu said. Arlo thought it was more like a drawstring bag.

The challenge was that everyone had to pull equally hard. Any slack and the piece would fall. But if anyone tugged too hard, the piece would flip or slip, then fall.

It was tough enough to get the first piece lifted, but walking with it was nearly impossible. Arlo was trudging backwards through the snow while keeping his elbows locked tight against his chest. The rope was cutting into his hands. He regretted taking off his gloves.

It took five minutes to move the first piece, but they managed to get it placed squarely on the platform. The second piece went faster. They were starting to get their rhythm, working together as a team. The third piece was trickier, because they needed to lift it into position. At the last moment, the twins' rope slipped. Jonas instinctively grabbed the piece as it fell.

The station captain whistled. It was a one-point deduction.

After a few frustrating moments, they got the fallen totem section out of the snow and up onto the pole. Arlo's arms were shaking with fatigue. He looped the rope around his hands, trying to get a better grip for the final piece.

"Slow and steady," said Connor. "Better it takes ten minutes than it slips."

As they slowly moved the last piece, Arlo's palms were sweating. He felt an odd tingle. A cramp? When he looked down, he found the rope wasn't coiled around his right hand anymore. But he still had a firm grasp, which was the important thing.

With agonizing precision, the patrol managed to place

the final piece. Arlo opened his fist to see the red imprint of the knot he had been squeezing.

While they waited for their official score, Indra and Arlo put back the ropes. "Wait, is this yours?" She held up his rope circle, showing him the simple overhand knot tied in it.

Arlo didn't remember the knot being there. "I guess. Why?"

"It's a knaught." She said it like the word was extremely important for some reason, but Arlo couldn't understand why.

"Yeah. It's a knot."

"No! Not *knot*. A *knaught*." That wasn't making it any more clear. She spelled it out instead. "K-N-A-U-G-H-T. It's a knot you can't tie, but you did somehow."

"I don't understand."

Wu came over, drinking from his water bottle. Indra enlisted his help, handing him another rope hoop.

"This rope is a circle, right? There are no free ends. But to tie an overhand knot like this, you need at least one free end."

"Wait," said Wu, suddenly excited. "Did he tie a knaught?"

"A slipknaught, I think." She handed Wu the rope. He handled it carefully, like it was a fragile artifact.

Arlo was starting to get it. A few knots, like the sheepshank, could be tied in the middle of a rope. But most knots required looping a free end through or around something. That wasn't possible with a circle of rope.

"How did you do it?" asked Wu.

"I don't know. It was an accident."

"Knaughts aren't even in the Field Book anymore," said Wu. "They took them out because they were too dangerous."

Indra shook her head. "They took them out because no one could tie them anymore. It's not even a requirement for Bear."

Wu looked to Indra. "We should open it."

"If anyone should, he should. He made it."

Wu handed Arlo the rope. "See if you can open it. Slowly."

Arlo carefully wiggled his fingers into the folds of rope. He could feel energy pulsing inside it. He looked up to find Wu and Indra had taken a step back.

"It's not going to blow up, is it?"

"No," said Indra with the slightest bit of a question mark. "But from everything I've heard, slipknaughts aren't stable, so . . ."

"It's going to be fine," said Wu. "Just maybe don't rush it."

"But don't dawdle, either. It could collapse at any point."

Arlo gently tugged at the edges of the knaught. As he did, he saw lines of light rippling through the fibers. His thumb slipped inside the loop—

—and disappeared.

It was very unsettling.

He could feel his thumb was still there. He could wiggle it, but he couldn't see it. It was invisible.

He pulled his thumb back and it reappeared, unharmed.

"Did you see that?" he asked.

"See what?" asked Wu.

The rope suddenly dropped open, the knaught untying itself. Whatever magic had formed it had dissipated.

"Guys!" shouted Connor. "Let's go!" He had returned to the sled with their completed route card. Arlo reluctantly dropped the rope circle and hurried back with Indra and Wu.

"We officially got nine points," said Connor. "The captain says only one team got ten."

Jonas perked up. "We could still beat Red. There's a chance."

As Arlo put his gloves back on, he rubbed the red spot on his palm where the knaught had dug in. It was still tingling.

"You okay?" asked Wu.

"I'm fine," said Arlo. "Let's beat Red."

26
134 DEGREES

AS THEY MERGED ONTO A BIGGER ROAD, Indra stopped the sled to check the map against her compass reading. "One hundred and thirty-four degrees. It's a straight shot. The finish line is less than a mile away."

Jonas pointed to the tracks in the snow. "Only two or three sleds have been through here. We're going to be one of the first. That's extra points."

"Let's get there before we worry about scores," said Connor.

Wu dropped the rope. "I'll be right back." He hurried off into the trees.

"Where are you going?" shouted Indra.

"I have to pee! I'm not going to make it a mile. You go ahead!"

"We never split the patrol," said Connor. "Just be quick."

Wu disappeared behind a suitable tree.

Julie dug her water bottle out of the sled. "Could we really beat Red Patrol?" she asked. "They were ahead of us."

"They beat us in the sprint, but we don't know what they got for sled-judging," said Indra. "That's ten points, too. The judges might have looked at their sled and decided they didn't really build it, whereas Mr. Henhao is clearly homemade."

Indra was the only kid Arlo had ever met who said "whereas." She sounded like a lawyer or a politician on TV. He could envision her standing at a podium, speaking in a half yell while gesturing with her hands for emphasis. If she was running for office, Arlo would vote for her. She was stubborn and intimidating, but also dedicated in a way most people weren't.

Arlo stopped paying attention as the others debated the theoretical point totals for the various patrols. He knew he had nothing to add to the conversation. He let his attention drift to the tops of the swaying pine trees, where the filtered sunlight split into rainbow colors.

"Nobody move," whispered Connor.

Arlo moved. He turned to look in the direction Connor was facing.

A giant bear lumbered into the road ahead of them. With each step, its massive body shifted and rolled. Its head turned, looking over at them. Its ears cocked forward, curious, but it stayed low to the ground.

Arlo froze. His heart pounded.

The Field Book spent several pages outlining the various species of bear, but suddenly Arlo couldn't remember any of it. This bear's fur was dark, but was it a brown bear? Black bear? Grizzly? He felt certain it wasn't a polar bear. Unless this was a very dirty polar bear—

"It's a grizzly," whispered Connor. "We need to back away quietly. Nobody run."

"Thunderclap!" whispered Jonas. "Scare it off."

"No! That will antagonize it," hissed Indra. "Just let it keep walking."

The bear turned to face them, sitting back on its haunches. It didn't seem interested in walking away.

Connor took charge. "Don't look it in the eye. Everyone grab the rope. We'll pull the sled the other way. Once we're out of sight, we'll figure out what to do."

Everyone nodded, slowly kneeling down to pick up the tow rope. Together, they carefully spun the sled to face the

opposite direction. The bear seemed interested but uncon-
cerned. Then—

"Guys!" shouted Wu, zipping his fly. "Finish line's that
way!"

He pointed directly at the bear. Off his friends' panicked
gaze, Wu followed his finger to see the massive bear rising
up on its back legs. It roared.

"Run!" shouted Jonas.

Arlo was pretty sure that was contrary to the directions in
the Field Book, which advised standing one's ground when
faced with an aggressive grizzly. But his feet weren't thinking. He was running as fast as he could, the rope looped in
the crook of his elbow.

Wu caught up to the sled, grabbing hold of it to steer.

Up ahead, the road split. "Left or right?" Arlo shouted.
Half the patrol answered each choice. Not helpful.

Meanwhile, the bear was charging. There was no way
they could outrun it.

Suddenly, a woman was standing in the middle of the
road. She wore a Warden's uniform, but looked too young to
be a parent of a Ranger. She held both hands out to her sides,
concentrating.

As she brought her arms to the sky, the snow on both sides
of the road suddenly swirled up into a blizzard. Howling

winds formed a complete whiteout except for a tiny passage around the sled. Here the air was calm. They were in the eye of the storm.

Wu uttered a combination of bad words that expressed his surprise. Whatever special Warden skill this was, they all wanted to learn it immediately.

Somewhere in the swirling snow, the bear roared in response.

The woman beckoned them to follow her. Quickly.

"Go!" Connor shouted.

She led the patrol off the road, winding through the trees. The Warden was remarkably fast, running more like a deer than a person. Arlo had a hard time keeping her in sight. She was always at the next bend, pointing exactly which way they should go.

Arlo looked back. He couldn't see the blizzard or the bear anymore. The woman seemed to be taking them well out of its territory. Better safe than sorry.

This part of the forest was different than the rest. It felt bigger. Older. They weaved between massive lichen-covered boulders, and crossed streams that had frozen solid. Even the bird songs were different.

A few minutes later, Arlo lost sight of the woman entirely. But he felt certain she must have headed towards the sunlit clearing ahead.

The sled slowed, then stopped. Arlo looked down and realized why. There was no snow under his boots, just wet dirt and pine needles.

One by one, the patrol gathered in a line at the front of the sled, staring in confused wonder. Wu pulled off his hat and gloves. He didn't need them anymore.

They were standing at the mouth of a shallow river valley. The white-capped mountains in the distance were taller than anything Arlo had ever seen. Ever imagined. They filled half the sky. The wind pulled curls of ice off the jagged peaks.

But here it was warm.

At the center of the clearing, a massive pine tree was burning. A coil of gray smoke rose from it, gradually dispersing in the purple sky. Flakes of ash drifted in the wind.

Through the flames, Arlo could see the skeleton of the tree, its glowing branches swaying in the heat of the fire. He could hear the flames crackling, whooshing.

But as fast as the tree was burning, it was also regrowing. New branches slowly reached out from the trunk, eventually igniting as other limbs collapsed into orange-white cinders.

It was a perfect equilibrium. A perpetual bonfire.

The burning tree was putting out so much heat that all the snow in the valley had melted.

Wu turned to the patrol. "Guys. Where are we?"

— 27 —

THE VALLEY OF FIRE

INDRA HELD OUT HER COMPASS. The patrol gathered around her to watch as the needle spun in a slow clockwise circle. North was everywhere, and nowhere.

They had crossed into the Long Woods.

"It was that woman, the Warden," said Wu. "She brought us here on purpose."

Indra snapped the compass shut. "She didn't talk. Did you guys notice that?"

"She didn't want to startle the bear," said Julie. Of the six of them, she seemed the least alarmed, like her brain hadn't quite caught up to how bad their situation was.

Connor unzipped his parka. "I'm not sure there ever was a bear. It could have all been an illusion."

"You think she's a witch?" asked Indra.

"Or something like it."

"Wait, there are witches?" asked Julie.

"Yes, but not vampires," said Arlo. "Which seems weird to me."

Jonas added his coat to the growing pile on the sled. "So let's say she's a witch—or like a witch. Why would she bring us here? To eat us?"

Connor, Wu and Indra looked over at Arlo. They didn't want to say it, so Arlo did: "She wanted me."

"Why?" asked Julie. "What's so special about you?"

There wasn't time to explain about the wisps and Connor's cousin and the Night Mare, so Indra just left it as, "We're not sure. But things keep trying to kill him."

"And this witch is probably the one who's been sending them," added Wu.

For weeks, Arlo had been feeling guilty about getting Connor, Indra and Wu involved. They were loyal friends who never complained, but this clearly wasn't their battle to fight. He suspected that just being near him put them in danger.

He felt even worse about Julie and Jonas, because they had been kept in the dark for months. They were part of the patrol, but not part of the inner circle. That felt disloyal and dishonest. And now the twins were lost in the Long Woods for reasons they couldn't understand.

255

Jonas pointed into the forest. "Look, we can just retrace our steps. Five minutes ago, we were in our world. We can go back."

"We can't," said Connor. "Directions don't work the same in the Long Woods."

"We don't need the compass!" said Julie. "The sled left a track. We'll just follow it until we're back."

Arlo shook his head. "It won't work. The tracks will disappear, or go in a circle."

"That's impossible."

"Yes, but so is that burning tree," said Indra. "So are those mountains. We're in an impossible place. It doesn't work the same as our world."

Jonas started walking back the way they came. "We can at least try. Seriously, what do we have to lose?"

"The minute you're out of sight, we'll never see you again," said Connor. "Trust me, I've been here before."

Indra's eyes narrowed. "Wait, here? Like here, here? This valley, with the pine tree?"

"I think so. Maybe." He took a step forward, surveying the meadow in front of them. "It all looks familiar, sort of the way a dream seems familiar. And it's not just the tree and the mountains. Over there, the moraine field—" He pointed at a slope covered with massive boulders. It looked like a cliff had been smashed by a giant fist. "I feel like I've been there. We hid in there for a while."

"Who? You and Katie?" asked Indra. Connor nodded. "What else do you remember?"

"There was a house. I remember knocking on the door. It swung open, like there wasn't even a lock."

"What was inside?"

Connor strained to remember, but came up with nothing. "Everything goes black after that. Next thing I knew, it was weeks later and I was in Canada. Katie was gone. They didn't want me. They only wanted her."

"Like they only want Arlo?" asked Julie. She was slowly coming up to speed. "If it's him they're after, maybe they'll let us go, too." As she said it, she deliberately didn't make eye contact with Arlo.

Indra was offended. "You can't be serious. We're not going to give up Arlo. He's our friend and fellow Ranger."

"So are we," said Jonas. "Yet somehow you didn't tell us anything about what was going on. We're here because of you, and because of him."

"We're not giving up Arlo," said Connor. "We're going to figure a way out of this together, as a patrol. No debate, no second-guessing. Understood?"

Jonas and Julie reluctantly nodded.

Wu had stayed out of the squabble. Now he pointed off to the distance, squinting. "Guys? There's something over there." He dug the binoculars out of the sled, focusing as he peered through them. "It's like a little stone cabin."

He handed them to Connor. Everyone waited for his verdict. He nodded slowly. "Yeah. That looks like the house I remember."

The binoculars were passed down the line. When it was finally Arlo's turn, he found himself disagreeing with both the terms *house* and *cabin*. The building in question was a circular pile of stones held together with mud. The roof was made of sagging wood and animal skins. A broken door hung askew in its frame.

This was at best a hut.

"We need to check it out," said Wu.

Indra scoffed. "You're kidding, right? It's obviously a trap. It couldn't be more of a trap if it had cheese and a giant spring. This witch, or like-a-witch, is waiting for us to go in there so she can catch us just like she caught Connor and Katie when they were little."

"She's right," said Arlo. "We can't go." Indra was happy to have someone else speaking common sense. But then Arlo continued. "I should go alone."

Connor dismissed that idea. "First rule of exploring: you never split the party."

"Unless you're sending a scout. That's in trailcraeft." Arlo had been reading ahead in the Field Book. "I'll be the scout. You guys stay here and build a ward around the sled. I don't know if it'll protect you, but it can't hurt." He took off his parka and perched it atop the others on the sled.

Indra tried to talk reason. "Arlo, you're obviously the one she wants. If you walk in there, she's got you. Then what? We're not any better off."

Jonas agreed. "We need you as a bargaining chip."

"That's not at all what I'm saying!" snapped Indra.

Wu focused on his friend. "Arlo, you can't go in there. If she sees you, you're dead or worse."

"She won't see me."

———•◦◉◦•———

Arlo untied the rope from the sled. He wasn't sure this would work, but something told him it was possible. From the moment they'd arrived in the valley, he'd felt something. A tingle on his skin. A buzz in his bones. At first, he thought it was just fear, but as the initial panic passed, the sensation only increased. The Long Woods had a vibration. Every tree, every leaf, every rock was humming.

And he was humming along with them.

He held a section of rope in his hands and began folding

it back on itself, twisting and gathering the loops. Indra was the first to recognize what he was trying to do. She motioned for everyone to give him space.

Unlike the bowline or two half hitches, there didn't seem to be an exact method for tying a knaught. It was more like art. You just kept working at it until you felt a change. Slowly, the rope became more supple, until he couldn't quite tell one loop from another. But his fingers never lost their place. They wove in and out, pushing and tugging.

Arlo closed his eyes, feeling as the fibers came alive. They started moving without being touched—but they were still under his command. The rope was heating up. He could smell it starting to scorch. So he slowed down. Took his time. A few more twists, then the final loops melted into place.

He opened his eyes. He opened his hands. There, tied in the middle of the rope, looked to be a simple overhand knot. On closer inspection, he could see tiny glimmers of light pulsing within the fibers.

He had tied a slipknaught. On purpose this time.

Indra was amazed. "How did you do that?"

"I don't know. It's like the rope moves through itself."

"It must be extra-dimensional," said Wu. "Think about it. You can't tie a normal knot like that in three dimensions, not without having one of the ends free. But if you had four dimensions, it would be easy." Realizing he had overstated it, he added, "Well, not easy, but possible."

Indra agreed. "Maybe that's why you can only tie knaughts in the Long Woods, and places close to it."

"Same with snaplights and thunderclaps," said Connor. "You have to bend space to do them."

"Snaplights and thunderclaps are useful," said Julie. She pointed at Arlo's rope. "How's that going to help anything?"

Arlo wiggled his fingers into the knaught, carefully pulling it open. As before, his thumbs disappeared. The space inside was shimmering like a soap bubble. He kept tugging at the edges to make the circle wider, until it was the size of a bicycle wheel. At every moment, he felt the knaught trying to squeeze itself shut. Gripping the rope tight, he stepped his right foot through the opening. His leg disappeared up to his thigh, yet he was still standing in front of them.

"Whoa," said Jonas, speaking for the group.

Arlo stepped his left foot into the opening. It too vanished, leaving him standing with only the upper half of his body visible. "I don't know how long this will last. You guys work on the ward."

"What do we do if she comes?" asked Wu.

Arlo looked to Connor. "Do a thunderclap. I'll hurry back."

"Wait!" said Indra. "I'm going with you."

Wu shot her a look. "You said it was a trap!"

"Which is why we can't let him go alone. He'll get himself killed." She put her hands on Arlo's shoulders, ready to step in. "Besides, if there's something important in there, I'm more likely to know what it is."

Arlo had to agree on that point.

He held the rope steady while Indra stepped in. It was a tight squeeze, but they both managed to fit inside. Then, with a flick, he pulled the loop over their heads. The knaught suddenly contracted as the rope fell to the ground. The fibers writhed, pulsing with energy.

Arlo and Indra had vanished.

— 28 —
THE HUT

THEY WERE THERE, BUT NOT THERE.

To their right, Wu and Julie were gathering red stones. Back at the sled, Connor and Jonas were sorting and stacking them to build the wards. Arlo and Indra could see their lips moving, but couldn't make out what they were saying.

"Why can't we hear them?" asked Indra.

Arlo thought back to summers swimming at the crowded pool in Philadelphia, how loud it was at the surface, and how quiet it was below. "I think it's like we're underwater."

Indra nodded—that's how it felt. Even the air seemed thicker, bending the light so it shimmered. Her hands sparkled as if dipped in glitter. She pointed to the rope on the ground, where the knaught was glowing brightly. "Should we take it with us? In case we need it again?"

Arlo reached down to pick it up. His fingers went right through the rope. Confused, he reached for the sled. His hand swept through the frame.

The slipknaught's enchantment had rendered them not just invisible, but intangible as well. They couldn't touch anything, nor be touched—yet they weren't falling through the ground to the center of the planet, so that was a plus.

Arlo thought about Cooper, stuck halfway between worlds, silently barking at things that weren't there. Maybe death was like a slipknaught that never untied.

The thought made him shudder. He and Indra had stepped through a hole into the land of the dead. Suddenly, this didn't seem like such a great idea.

At least he wasn't alone.

"We should go," said Indra. "We don't know how long we have." Arlo agreed. He hoped the effects would last more than a few minutes, but less than forever.

Walking felt normal, except every footstep was silent. As they approached the pine tree, Arlo and Indra could see the individual needles burning. Glowing red, then white, they curled up on themselves before finally crumbling into ash.

Indra tried to catch one as it fell, but it passed right through her hand.

The hut was just ahead. It sat in the middle of a riverbed, where a tiny stream of melted snow spilled across rocks. Dragonflies flitted from puddle to puddle. Animal bones and carcasses were scattered among the smooth stones, garbage tossed aside after a meal.

Indra pointed to the door. It was swinging slightly, like it had just been opened. But it could have also been the wind.

They carefully approached. There was enough of a crack between the door and the frame that Arlo could peer inside. Indra leaned on his shoulder, straining to get a look as well.

The hut was a single room with a mud floor. No windows, no real furniture, just a filthy mattress with hay poking out of it. A heavy kettle hung over the ashes of a fire. Other than the door, the only light came from a rip in the ceiling. *Definitely not a cabin*, Arlo thought.

Suddenly, a shape moved past. Indra gasped and tucked behind the wall. Arlo fell on his butt.

The woman had been standing in the one spot in the hut they couldn't see. She slowly turned towards Arlo. For a moment, he was sure she saw him. But her eyes never focused on him. The slipknaught's enchantment seemed to be working.

He carefully sat up, leaning close to the door.

The woman was no longer dressed as a Warden. Instead, she wore a dirty blue summer dress that was tattered at the edges. Despite the state of her clothes, she was undeniably beautiful: tall and strong, like the women on magazine covers. She seemed to be lit by an inner glow. Arlo felt he could watch her for hours and never look away.

She was speaking—but to whom? He was pretty sure there was no one else in the hut. Because of the enchantment, he couldn't hear what she was saying. Not that he necessarily would have been able to understand it anyway.

Indra whispered, though she probably didn't need to. "That thing in her hand. It's a speakshell. I've read about them." The woman brought a spiral conch to her ear, as if listening to the ocean. "They come as matched pairs. Anything you say into one gets whispered out the other, like a tin-can phone without the string."

Arlo remembered making one, except with two plastic cups and dental floss. "She's talking to somebody. Maybe telling them that we're here."

"Or getting instructions about what to do next." As if on cue, the woman put the shell to her ear again.

"What do you think she is?" asked Arlo.

"If I had to guess, I'd say she's a hag. It's like a forest witch. That's definitely not her real form."

"How do you know?"

"Look at her feet. She's barefoot, but her feet are completely clean. It's all an illusion."

Suddenly, the woman—the hag—was finished with her

call. She tucked the shell into a dark nook inside the wall, then headed for the door. Arlo and Indra tucked back so she wouldn't walk right through them.

"We need to follow her," said Arlo.

"Wait. She's not headed for the sled." Indra was right. The hag was squatting over a puddle. They watched as she began pulling a net out of the water. It was much bigger than they would have imagined possible. As she tugged it up, she picked off crawdads and urchins, smashing them between rocks.

Arlo's eyes narrowed. "I think she's hungry."

"Good. We have a few minutes." Indra stepped into the hut before he could object. Arlo decided to follow her. If the enchantment wore off, at least they'd be out of sight.

The area of the hut they hadn't seen was the most interesting. A crude shelf held various herbs and ingredients. Some of the jars were clearly from the normal world, with faded supermarket labels reading THYME or ROSEMARY. But inside were swirling beetles, spiders, or sand. Indra tried to pick one up, forgetting that her fingers couldn't grab anything.

At the back of the hut, a cage hung from the roof by a rope. It was made of thin branches rather than wire, but in most ways resembled the home of a parrot or cockatiel. It was wrapped with a dirty cloth, except for the lowest few inches.

Arlo leaned in to look. The bottom of the cage was littered with cracked bones. They weren't just stripped of the meat. They had been split open, the marrow sucked dry.

Suddenly, the cage shook. It swung on the rope, spinning. Arlo backed away as the cloth fell off the cage. The hut was now brightly lit.

Two wisps floated in the cage. They rammed themselves against the wooden slats, futilely trying to get at Arlo.

His panic returned, heart beating in his throat. "They can see us! We're not invisible."

Indra carefully approached the cage. She moved her hand along the far side. The wisps paid her no attention. "I don't think they can really see us. But they sense you're here. It's like they've been trained to find you."

Arlo peeked out the door. The hag was still hunched over the puddle, picking through her net. For all their fury, the wisps evidently weren't making enough sound to attract her attention. "She was the one who sent them. That night in the forest, they were looking for me specifically."

"I think so." Indra looked around. "We need to keep searching. There might be—" She stopped short, unsettled.

They both felt it. Something was happening.

If the slipknaught was like being underwater, this was like surfacing. With an audible whoosh, the enchantment came to an abrupt end. They felt themselves shoved back into the ordinary world—or at least the extraordinary world of the Long Woods.

Their skin was no longer shimmering. They were visible again.

A bit dizzy, Arlo carefully made his way to the door to check on the hag. "She's still there."

"Let's keep looking. Maybe we can find something useful."

By the light of the wisps, it was clear the walls were riddled with pockets and niches. They found tin necklaces, long needles, bird skulls and marbles.

High on the wall where he couldn't quite see, Arlo's fingers touched something soft. Cloth. He pulled it down. It was yellow, the color of supermarket mustard. Even before he unfolded it, he knew what it was.

His uncle's neckerchief. He recognized the dried blood-stain.

Indra took it from him. She checked the logo, confused. "It's from Pine Mountain Company."

"It was my uncle's. He lent it to me. I had it at the first meeting, but then I couldn't find it afterwards."

It was never lost, Arlo thought. *It was taken.*

"But that's impossible," said Indra. "We never had a Yellow Patrol."

Arlo couldn't explain it. "He said it was his."

On a hunch, Indra held the neckerchief near the cage. The wisps immediately frenzied, desperate to get it.

"They're like bloodhounds," she said. "They're trained on the scent, or something like a scent. That's how they sensed you even when they couldn't see you."

She handed him back the neckerchief. He was tucking it into his cargo pocket when—

BOOM! A thunderclap.

Arlo looked back outside. The hag was gone.

— 29 —
TOOBLE

THE WINDS HAD SHIFTED.

Smoke from the burning tree was now drifting across the valley floor. Arlo squinted, his eyes stinging. He couldn't see the hag. He couldn't see his friends back at the—

BOOM! Another thunderclap.

They were in trouble.

Arlo and Indra ran towards the sound. The smoke kept getting thicker, scratching their throats, burning their lungs.

Indra pulled off her neckerchief, dipping it in one of the dirty puddles. She held it to her mouth, breathing through it. She gave a thumbs-up—it helped. Arlo followed her example, plunging his own neckerchief into the muck. The wet fabric smelled like pond scum and gym socks. But it worked. He could breathe again.

They pressed onward through the smoke. As they passed the burning tree, all they could see was a glowing orange smudge. But they were close. The edge of the woods—and the patrol—had to be just ahead.

Suddenly, the wind shifted again, lifting the smoke up like a bedsheet. Surprised to find themselves suddenly exposed, Arlo and Indra dropped to the dirt, crawling behind a flat rock.

The hag stood just twenty feet away, her back to them. The fishing net was tied around her waist like a sash. Their friends huddled behind the sled. Connor shielded Julie and Jonas, warning them, "Don't look her in the eye!" Wu kept his gaze down, but held the chili pot as a weapon.

Indra pointed to the stacked stones. "The wards are working," she whispered. "She can't get any closer."

Indeed, the hag seemed to be blocked by an invisible wall. She began circling the sled, one hand feeling for cracks in the protection. As she moved, the patrol sidestepped in the opposite direction, always keeping the maximum distance from her. They were careful not to bump into the wards.

Although the hag appeared to be human, there was something otherworldly about how she moved. Each step was too big, each gesture exaggerated. She seemed to still be learning how to use this body.

Wu spotted Arlo and Indra. They motioned with fingers to their mouths—quiet. He nodded.

The hag completed her circle, still no closer to getting in. "They're safe," Arlo whispered.

"Those wards won't last forever. We need to find a way to stop her."

With a sudden idea, Arlo reached into his right cargo pocket, feeling for the familiar glass container. He pulled it out: his salt shaker.

"What is that for?"

"Maybe I can dispel her like the Night Mare."

"That won't work. She wasn't summoned. This is her home." She tugged on her ear. Arlo recognized that this meant she was thinking, so he stayed quiet. Still, he wasn't ready to give up on the salt. He had been carrying it for weeks, anticipating just such an emergency. Maybe it could work as a distraction. Nobody likes having salt thrown on them. Even hags, he presumed.

Indra began emptying her own pockets. Arlo hadn't realized she had been grabbing all the items she found in the hut. She held up a dirty glass jar with holes punched in its rusted lid. "This might do it." Inside, three iridescent bugs scuttled about. "Faerie beetles."

Arlo took the jar, marveling at the strange insects. He now understood why Wu had been trying to catch one the day they met. They shimmered, never quite one color.

The hag knelt down in front of the sled. She pressed her fingers into the dirt. But they weren't fingers anymore. They were claws. The hag was reverting to her true form: Leathery blue skin covered with scars. A tangle of black hair. Two bone-white horns jutting from her forehead.

The earth around the hag's hands began churning, roiling. Then the ground began to shake. Arlo had never felt an actual earthquake, but he was sure this was one.

The stacked stones that formed the wards began to rattle. Connor suddenly realized the hag's plan. "Don't let them fall over!"

Connor, Wu, Jonas and Julie frantically tried to keep the little towers upright. But the tremors were too strong. One by one, the stones toppled. The wards had fallen.

"Run!" Connor shouted. "Run for the rocks! Hide!" He pushed them ahead.

The hag slowly stood. As she craned her neck, her human form reemerged in stages. First her hands, then her legs, finally her face. She smiled darkly. She was enjoying this.

With one smooth motion, the hag pulled the net from her waist and flung it at Jonas as he ran. It tripped him. He fell hard. The net's magical fibers began creeping up his legs like a spider wrapping its prey. He screamed in panic.

Wu and Connor doubled back to help him. With their pocketknives, they began sawing through the threads. With each one they cut, two more took its place. It was futile.

Indra grabbed Arlo's arm. "Throw it!"

He'd completely forgotten he was holding the faerie beetles. Standing up, Arlo took careful aim and threw the jar at the hag with all his might.

He missed.

The jar sailed right past her, landing in the dirt beside Wu.

The hag turned, spotting Arlo. She suddenly lost interest in the others. "Tooble!" she said, her smile growing impossibly wide.

This was her. This was the voice he had heard calling from the forest.

Arlo backed away as she approached.

Indra stepped in front of him as a shield, keeping her gaze low. "I won't let you hurt him."

Arlo pushed her aside. "Just run. She only wants me." He stood his ground. With no plan other than buying his friends some time, he looked the hag directly in the eye.

Suddenly, everything was okay.

No, better than that. Better than it had ever been.

Arlo found himself back in his almost-too-soft bed, watching the morning sun glisten off the faded snowflake-flowers on the wallpaper. He could smell pancakes with maple syrup, but he was too lazy to get out of bed. He stretched his hand to reach the bell of his Zephyr Fireball Maxx. *Ding!*

A knock. He looked over as his mom opened the door. "Are you going to sleep all day?" she asked with a smile. With a hand on her shoulder, Arlo's dad pushed the door open a little further. "Let him rest. We've got a big ride this afternoon. Ten miles!" Arlo flicked the lever on the bell. *Ding!*

Cooper looked up from the foot of the bed, where he always slept.

"Arlo?" the dog asked. "Arlo!" Funny, Cooper had never spoken before. He'd had no idea his dog spoke with a girl's voice. Cooper seemed upset. That wasn't like him at all.

With a growl, Cooper suddenly bit his hand.

Arlo looked down at the wound. A drop of blood rose to the surface. He looked up to see Indra standing beside him in the valley, one of the hag's needles in her hand. "Arlo! Run!" she shouted.

He knew he should move. Hide. Indra was smart, and stubborn, and almost always right. But it was so much easier to just stay put. His parents were there, together, standing in the doorway. If he could just allow himself to believe the illusion, everything would be wonderful.

"Guys!" shouted Wu. "Duck!"

Arlo turned to look just as Wu threw the glass jar. It hit the side of the hag's head, shattering. The panicked faerie beetles immediately sprayed the contents of their unctuous bladders. Upon contact with air, the clear liquid transformed into a sticky purple goo.

Some got on Arlo's uniform. Some got in Indra's hair. But most of it coated the hag's face, blinding her. She roared so loudly it echoed through the valley.

Arlo's trance was broken. He was back in his body, back in the valley. He started running for the rocky slope, Indra right beside him.

Connor cut through the net entangling Jonas—it had stopped repairing itself. Wu helped them up. All three boys raced for the moraine field, where Julie was already scrambling up the giant rocks.

Still blinded, the hag howled, thrusting her arms to the sky. As she did, the ground moved again. Twisted wooden spikes erupted from the dirt, each as long as a spear. Arlo recognized them from the pit he'd nearly fallen into when chasing the wisps. No one had dug it. The hag had formed it magically.

"They're roots!" shouted Indra. "They're the roots of the tree."

Indeed, each of the long spikes was tipped with a glowing

ember. As they shot up, they crisscrossed to form crude barricades.

The hag couldn't see her prey, but she could stop them from getting away.

The spikes kept coming, wave after wave. The only hope was to dodge them and avoid being impaled. Arlo zigged left while Indra zagged right. They were just ten feet apart, but separated by a dozen smoldering posts, each covered in barbs.

He tripped, rolling to the side just as a new spike burst from the dirt.

"Get to the rocks!" shouted Connor. "It's safe there!" He was right: the spikes were only coming out of the valley floor. The rocks were protected. Arlo eyed a path that could take him there. It was only a hundred feet away, but every few steps, he needed to veer left or right as new spikes shot up.

With a final leap, he scrambled up onto a rock the size of his desk at school. He looked back, astonished to see how dense the field of spikes had become. Beyond them, the hag was still writhing, trying to clear the purple goo from her eyes.

To his right, he saw Connor, Wu and Jonas all safely off the valley floor. Julie was already tucking into the space between two rocks. But he couldn't find Indra anywhere.

"Arlo!" she shouted. She was close. He finally spotted her, boxed in by a dozen spikes. She had nowhere to go.

He made his way over to her, careful to stay up on the rocks. "You can climb through over here," he shouted, pointing to the V formed by two crossing posts.

"I can't get up there! It's too high." Just then, another spike shot up behind her. She was nearly skewered.

Pulling her hair back, Indra steadied herself. She examined the spikes in front of her. There was simply no way through them. But she suddenly had an idea.

Indra pulled her belt from her trousers and wrapped it around one of the barbed posts. Gripping the leather tight, she placed one boot up on the pole. The next one, higher. Arlo watched as Indra jumped the belt up a few inches and repeated the process, slowly making her way up like a lumberjack climbing a pole.

The trickiest part was the transition. She stepped her left foot into the V, praying it would hold her. Then she swung her weight over. There was nothing left to do but—

"Jump! I'll catch you!" shouted Arlo.

Abandoning her belt, Indra leaped. Arlo didn't so much catch her as provide a landing pad. Both fell back on the rocks, rattled but unhurt.

"Keep climbing!" shouted Connor. "Spread out!"

Arlo looked up at the rocky slope above him. It was as

wide as a football field, filled with nooks and pockets. That made it the perfect place to hide. And hiding seemed to be their only hope.

———•◦•———

As he wedged himself into the narrow gap beneath a boulder, Arlo was suddenly glad to be the smallest kid in Rangers. It just might keep him alive.

The rocks were slick from melting snow. He could feel the cold soaking through the back of his uniform as he inched his way deeper.

From this angle, he could only see the top of the ever-burning pine tree as it sent a coil of smoke rising into the purple sky. He could only hear the blood rushing in his ears.

Maybe they had gotten away. Maybe the hag was searching the forest, rather than the rocky slope. Maybe—

"Tooble! Tooooo-ble!" Her voice was like a rusty hinge. It was the same way you would call a dog to dinner. Except Arlo was the meal.

Exhaling, Arlo squeezed further into the crevice. A small orange lizard suddenly darted out, annoyed by this intruder. Each of the creature's three eyes blinked in succession, studying the boy. Arlo made a mental note to look up the lizard when he got home.

If he got home.

To his right, he heard claws on the rocks. The hag was close. Arlo's perfect hiding spot now seemed far less ideal. He had left himself no escape path. Either she would find him or she wouldn't, and there was nothing he could do.

A woman's bare foot stepped into view, the tattered edge of her filthy dress draping across her calf. Her skin was clean and smooth as marble.

At the edge of the rocks, the three-eyed lizard stared up, transfixed—until a clawed hand suddenly snatched it up. Arlo listened as the hag crunched through the lizard's bones, finishing it with a slurp.

Whatever enchantment the hag was using to appear beautiful was interrupted by her eating. Arlo watched as the hag's ankles turned deep blue, with boils and scars erupting. Worms slithered just beneath the skin. Her toenails were actually jagged black talons, scraping on the stones.

With a groan, she was gone. Arlo could only guess that she had climbed on top of the boulder to get a better view of the moraine field.

Arlo knew he needed to stay put. As seconds turned to minutes, he started to shiver, as much from adrenaline as from the cold. His left foot was going numb. Plus he couldn't really breathe.

To distract himself, Arlo silently mouthed the words to the Vow:

Loyal, brave, kind and true—
Keeper of the Old and New—
I guard the wild,
Defend the weak,
Mark the path,
And virtue seek.
Forest spirits hear me now
As I speak my Ranger's Vow.

Arlo smiled. It was the first time he had gotten the right words in the right order.

Assuming he escaped the hag, and found his friends, and somehow made it out of the Long Woods—assuming he survived at all—he would earn Squirrel rank for sure.

But first, he needed to move. He couldn't risk staying in this spot any longer. The icy water seeping through the rocks would eventually lead to hypothermia. He needed to find somewhere drier to hide.

He very slowly began to inch his way towards the light. His shirt buttons caught on a tiny ledge of rock. There wasn't room to wedge his fingers in to help, so he exhaled completely, sucking in his chest. That did it. He wiggled his way past the obstacle and took a deep breath.

Arlo listened for claws. For footsteps. For grit sliding between the rocks. There was nothing but the wind. If the hag was close, she was completely silent.

He reached his hand around the edge of the rock.

Then he heard it: the tinkling bells of a cat's collar. The sound of the purple goo. He froze.

It was close. It had to be the hag, except—funny, he hadn't heard it when she was standing right there. Maybe she had magically rid herself of the goo.

Then why was he hearing it now?

He slowly pulled his arm back under the rock. Again, he heard the jingling. It was coming from him. He turned his cuff around to find the spot of purple goo on his sleeve. He sighed with relief. Then—

A scream. It was a girl. Julie, not Indra. She was far away.

Arlo scooted the rest of the way out, trying to get his bearings. It was starting to rain—snow, actually, but it melted as it fell, forming a fine mist.

"Help! Somebody!" The voice was coming from down the slope. He climbed up on a boulder, surveying the field. Connor was nearby. He spotted Wu about halfway down, trying to find a way up.

Then he saw the hag. She was far down the slope, dragging Julie by the hair. They were atop a flat boulder.

A thunderclap. The hag looked up at Connor, curious. He shot three snaplights at her. They didn't hurt, but they distracted her enough that Julie was able to wriggle free, escaping back down between the rocks.

Another snaplight whipped past, this time from a different direction. It had to be Jonas. Then a third—which fell short. Indra. Wu was trying too, but the light never left his fingers.

"Keep trying!" shouted Connor. "Distract her!"

Arlo looked at his dirty hand. He had no idea if he could actually throw a snaplight. He'd never even gotten a shimmer. But he had to try.

He cocked his arm like he was pitching a baseball. As his hand rose, he felt a tingle, like static electricity. It was the same energy he sensed in the rope when he was tying the knaught, only this time it was inside him.

He pressed his thumb to his third finger.

A spark. A rush. Arlo could sense the air bending around him.

In one smooth motion, his elbow straightened. His hand flicked forward. His index finger pointed directly at the hag.

And he snapped.

The light was blinding, like a camera flash in a dark

room. It crackled as it left his fingertip, tracing a straight line through the air. It didn't arc. It was too fast. Too strong.

He could see the mist ripple, a radiant crease in the air.

The bolt hit the hag square in the chest, blasting her off the rock. Arlo watched as she fell out of sight.

He looked at his hand in disbelief. A snaplight shouldn't do that. It was just light, after all—no heat, no force. Yet it had hit her like a cannonball.

"What was that?!" shouted Wu.

"I don't know."

The air smelled like lightning. Arlo checked his fingertips. They were raw and red from climbing the rock, but not scorched. He had no idea how he'd done it, or if he could ever do it again.

Down the slope, Julie carefully climbed up on the boulder, looking over the edge. "Guys! Come down here!"

Arlo and the rest of the patrol made their way down to her. Other than scrapes and bruises, none of them were hurt. Arlo was the last to arrive at the edge of the moraine field. The last to see what had happened.

The hag had fallen on one of her spikes. It had skewered her through the chest, leaving her dangling helplessly a few feet off the ground.

There was no blood. The wound was completely dry.

In fact, everything about the forest witch seemed

desiccated. Her blue skin was rough as bark. Her fingers looked like bent twigs.

"She's turning into wood," said Indra. Arlo could see she was right. The change had started in her chest, but was quickly spreading. In a few moments, she would transform completely.

The hag's dark eyes—fast becoming tree knots—fixed on Arlo. He stepped closer, unafraid. He felt a mix of pity and disgust.

"Why were you trying to kill me?" he asked.

The hag smiled, a few teeth falling out. She lifted her twig hand, pointing at Arlo's mismatched eyes.

"Tooble," she whispered.

And then she was gone. Arlo could feel her spirit depart, leaving behind just a wooden husk. Whatever answers the hag might have had, she took them with her.

— 30 —
THE WAY BACK

THE HAG WAS GONE.

With her passing, the spiky roots began retreating back into the dirt, leaving small pockmarks across the valley floor. As it descended, the hag's wooden body cracked into pieces, indistinguishable from common kindling.

The pine tree kept burning. Its magic was apparently independent of hers. The fire that had seemed so menacing was now almost comforting. It reminded Arlo of that first campfire at Ram's Meadow, back before all their lives were in peril.

Standing around the sled, the patrol drank from their water bottles. Connor gathered the ward stones, just in case.

Indra reattached the rope. The twins rinsed their scrapes and applied bandages.

No one spoke. They were too exhausted, too keyed up.

Wu finished the last of his water. He screwed the cap back on. "Guys?" he asked. "How do we get out of here?"

They were all thinking the same thing. While the hag had been the immediate threat, the bigger concern was geography. They were in the wrong world, without any idea how to get back to their own.

Julie spoke first. "We need to stay put. That's what our parents taught us when we were little. When you're lost in the woods, you look for an open space and stay there. That way, the search parties can find you."

"Like they found Connor and Katie?" asked Indra. She immediately regretted her tone. Julie was close to tears. "I'm sorry. It's just that no one knows we're in the Long Woods. We can't expect anyone to find us here. At least, not anyone we want to find us."

"What do you mean?" asked Connor.

Indra traded a look with Arlo. "In the hut, we saw the hag talking with someone. Magically—they weren't there in person. But there's definitely someone else involved. It's safe to assume they're on their way."

"Then we have to go," said Connor. "We'll climb to the top of the valley and scout it out. Pick a direction and go."

"What about the sled?" asked Wu.

"We leave it here. Carry what we can."

Wu was aghast. "We're not giving up Mr. Henhao! He's part of the patrol."

Jonas rolled his eyes. "It's a busted chair and old skis. Get over it."

"We came in second!" shouted Wu. "That's really good."

"At least we made something, Jonas," said Indra. "What have you two ever done, other than complain and get rescued?"

Connor got between them. "Enough! All of you."

The patrol went silent. Julie was now freely crying. She shrugged off her brother's attempt to comfort her. "It's hopeless," she said, shaking her head. "We're going to die here, aren't we?"

"No, we're not," said Arlo. "I can get us home."

While his friends were arguing, Arlo had pulled out his compass. The needle was still spinning in a slow circle. But as he turned, he felt something: the slightest buzz. It wasn't north. It was something else altogether.

Back when he was practicing on his driveway, he had learned to ignore the phantom vibrations. Now he realized they were indicating something real: paths into the Long Woods.

Here, standing in the Woods, the compass was showing him the way back out.

"How sure are you?" asked Connor. "On a scale of one to ten."

Arlo was honest. "Maybe a six or a seven. I know something is there, but I can't be sure."

"For all we know, it's pointing him deeper into the Woods," said Jonas. "If he's wrong, we're worse off than before."

" 'Worse' is probably on its way right now," said Indra. "We can't stay here. It's too dangerous."

Wu stepped forward. "Why are we even discussing this? Look what Arlo did with the rope! Look what he did with the snaplight! None of us could do that. Not me, not you, not Connor. Even Christian couldn't do that. I bet those firecraefters at the bonfire last night, they couldn't do that. No one can do what Arlo can do. So if he says he thinks he can get us out of here, guess what? I believe him. I don't need to know why or how. I just need to know which direction to pull the sled, because he's going to get us home, simple as that."

Indra turned to Arlo. So did Connor. Even the twins faced him. The argument was over.

Wu gestured at Arlo's compass. "Which way are we headed?"

Arlo pointed. It wasn't the same direction they'd come from, but it was where he felt the vibration.

"Okay! Let's go." Wu took his jacket off the sled, putting it on and zipping it up. One by one, the rest of the patrol grabbed their coats. Then, on a count of three, they picked up the sled, carrying it to the nearest snow.

Wrapping the towrope around his glove, Arlo took one last look back at the valley and the burning tree. How long had he been here? An hour? Two? He felt like there was so much more to explore. But it was time to go home.

Once they started moving, they were quickly back in their rhythm. Arlo could hear skis and boots on the snow.

In the normal world, Rangers used their compasses to pick a distant landmark—a specific tree, a mountaintop, a boulder—and head towards it in a straight line. While you were walking, the compass could go back in your pocket. But in the Long Woods, that didn't work. Here, there were no straight lines. The paths were always twisting. Every few steps, Arlo could feel the vibration shifting. It could be as small a change as passing a fallen log on the right or the left.

Pick wrong, and you've lost the trail. There was no going back.

At the front of the rope, Arlo couldn't see the others' faces, but he was sure they were skeptical of his route. He would be, too. At one point, they made a hard right followed by a hard left in what looked to be an ordinary stretch of trees. But as they came over a small rise, they found the path had taken them somewhere remarkable.

A bridge of solid ice spanned a fast-moving river. It looked just wide enough for the sled, no margin of error. Falling in was not an option: just to the left, the water plunged off a massive cliff. You could see for miles—hundreds of miles, maybe—to a spot where the purple sky met the horizon in a pink-orange glow.

All around them, icicles clung to the trees, sparkling in the light. Julie held up her hands like a frame. "I wish I had my camera."

"I'm sure cameras don't work here," said Connor. "Otherwise, you'd see photos from the Long Woods all the time."

Indra agreed. "It's like the Wonder times ten."

Jonas pointed out the obvious: "We definitely didn't cross this bridge before."

"I know," said Arlo. "But this is the way back. I can feel it."

Wu picked up the towrope. "Good enough for me. Nobody fall in."

For a bridge made of solid ice, it was less slippery than Arlo had feared. The frozen spray from the river offered some traction under their boots. And they weren't the first to cross it that day. Indra spotted tracks in the frost. "A hexlynx," she said. "See how it has six legs? I bet it's hiding in the trees right now, watching us."

After one heart-stopping moment where the sled drifted dangerously close to the edge, they made it across safely. Arlo led them over the next rise. A minute later, he stopped, confused.

"Which way?" asked Connor.

"I don't know. It's gone."

"What do you mean, 'gone'?" asked Jonas. "Are we lost?"

"I don't know! It feels different."

Indra pulled out her own compass. "It's not spinning anymore! I don't think we're in the Long Woods."

Connor pulled out his compass to check.

Arlo quickly raced back the way they'd come. As he came to the top of the small rise, he saw nothing but ordinary trees. The river and the ice bridge were gone. "She's right!" he yelled. "We're back!"

"But where are we, exactly?" asked Jonas.

"I don't want to be in Canada," said Julie.

Wu had wandered away from the sled, looking for something in the trees. Suddenly, his eyes went wide. "Guys! Guys! Come here!" As they approached, he explained. "This is where we saw the bear. Remember, I was taking a leak? This is the tree I was peeing on."

"How do you know?" asked Indra.

"Because I always write my initials." He pointed down, where *HW* was marked in yellow snow. "Henry Wu."

"You're disgusting," she said, hugging him.

Connor checked his watch. "It's not even four o'clock yet. We can still finish."

The six members of Blue Patrol looked at one another for a long moment. After surviving the bear, the hag and the Long Woods, they had completely forgotten about the Alpine Derby.

They were exhausted. They needed to eat and sleep. This was no time for pointless pride.

Julie spoke first. "Let's do it. Let's beat Red."

— 31 —
THE FINISH LINE

IT WAS GETTING DARK. The shadows on the snow had faded, leaving only an indistinct gray. A cold wind was rising. Arlo zipped his parka up to his chin. The metal teeth bit into his skin a bit, but he didn't mind. The irritation distracted him from his aching feet and sticky eyes, still stinging from the smoke in the valley.

Even without the compass, he was certain they were headed in the right direction. He could see dozens of ski tracks in the snow. But the road seemed endless.

They could hear it before they could see it. Just around the bend, a hundred Rangers and adults were cheering and banging drums. They were almost there.

"Let's run the last part," said Connor. Everyone agreed.

Summoning their last reserves of energy, the Rangers of Blue Patrol came around the final turn of the forty-ninth annual Alpine Derby in a full sprint.

Twenty-eight of the thirty patrols had already finished. They were mingling around the bonfire and drinking hot chocolate. A girl from Green was the first to spot Blue Patrol emerging from the forest. She rallied a bunch of Rangers to cheer for them. It felt a bit like pity.

A few of the Red Patrol members looked over. They stayed quiet.

The finish line was a bright red board in the snow. Blue Patrol didn't stop running until the sled was fully across it.

They were sweaty, cold and beyond exhausted. Arlo wanted to fall asleep in a hot bath. But there was one more thing to do.

Connor waved them together into a huddle. They leaned in, putting their heads together. "Last time," he said. "Everything we've got."

They lined up. Arlo was back on the end, the smallest Ranger. Voices hoarse, they yelled:

Clap your hands!
Stomp your feet!
Blue Patrol just can't be beat!
Faster than a snowshoe hare,

Stronger than a grizzly bear.
Both tomorrow and today,
Blue Patrol will lead the way!

———•◦•———

As they were drinking their second cups of hot chocolate, Indra came over to Arlo and Connor. "I found this in the hut. Didn't want the others to know."

She handed Connor a tarnished silver necklace. A tiny pendant had the initials *KC*.

Connor recognized it. "It was Katie's. I don't remember her wearing it, but it was in all the missing persons bulletins. Her grandfather gave it to her." He tried to hand it back.

"No. You should have it."

Connor shrugged. "She should have it. I'll give it to her parents." He tucked it into his jacket pocket. "But I don't know if she'll take it. She doesn't like anyone calling her Katie. She says that was never her real name."

Arlo had to keep reminding himself that to Connor, his cousin wasn't missing. She was just living abroad in another country that happened to be another world. Connor was used to it. He had been keeping the secret so long that it no longer felt like a secret.

They looked over as the last patrol crossed the finish line.

It was time for the results. As all the Rangers gathered near the bonfire, they met up with Wu, Julie and Jonas.

"I've been asking around, and I think there's a chance we came in third," said Wu. "Not third in the company, but third out of everyone."

Arlo was confused. "How is that possible? We were the next to last patrol to finish."

"You get four points just for crossing the finish line," said Indra, counting on her fingers. "Plus three points for visiting the stations in order, which we did. That's seven out of ten points. The first team to cross could have only gotten three more than us."

"Which they didn't," said Wu. "Red was the first across, but they went to Signaling before Knots, so they lost those three points. And I hear they messed up in Knots. They did a sheet bend instead of a sheepshank."

"Man, I would love to beat them," said Jonas.

Julie shook her head. "I just want to place. After everything we went through today, I just want to be in the top three."

"It's going to come down to spirit," said Indra. "We know we have eighty-one points. Last year, third place was ninety. If we get nine out of ten, we could do it."

The bearded Warden climbed up on a stepladder. In daylight, Arlo could see tattoos on his neck, mostly hidden by his giant beard. The crowd quieted. The man called out, "Rangers! May your path be safe!"

In unison, everyone responded, "May your aim be true!"

"Forty-eight years ago, the first Rangers raced these mountains. They called it the Alpine Derby. It was not a race of miles and minutes, but of will and conviction, meant to test the ideals of the Ranger's Vow: loyalty, bravery, kindness and truth. For while the obstacles are ever-changing, the virtues with which we confront them are eternal."

Arlo thought back to the valley, and their battle with the hag. It wasn't knaughts and snaplights that had saved their lives. It was working together. None of them were perfectly loyal, brave, kind or true—but they didn't need to be. Between the six members of Blue Patrol, there was enough loyalty, bravery, kindness and truth to go around.

The Warden looked down to his clipboard. "We had thirty patrols racing this year. Congratulations to everyone who finished. It's now time to call out the top three patrols for flags."

Indra grabbed Arlo's and Wu's hands. This was it. If they were getting any award, this was their shot. Arlo held his breath.

"Finishing third, with ninety points, is Moose Patrol of Cheyenne Company."

A cheer went up. Arlo looked over as a group of Wyoming

Rangers made their way up to the ladder. One of the boys was blind and held his friend's sleeve as they walked. The Warden handed them a black flag embroidered with copper thread. They held it high and yelled their patrol cheer.

Arlo couldn't even process the words. He sank deep into himself, disappointed in ways that surprised him. Just a few minutes earlier, he hadn't considered the possibility of getting third place. Now that it was gone, the loss stung.

He silently vowed to never want anything again. To never be overly hopeful. It hurt too much.

Arlo accidentally crossed gazes with Russell Stokes. Russell traced a fake tear down his cheek, mouthing *boo-hoo*.

Wu caught the exchange. "Ignore him. He's a jerk."

Arlo shook it off. It was stupid to be upset about losing a third-place flag after nearly being killed.

As Moose Patrol stepped to the side, the Warden climbed the ladder again. "In second place, with ninety-one points, is Blue Patrol of Pine Mountain Company."

Arlo didn't hear it right. He assumed the Warden had said "Green Patrol" or "Red Patrol." But then he saw Indra and Wu jumping up and down. Connor was stunned, wide-eyed. Jonas and Julie were screaming.

"We must have gotten a perfect ten in spirit," said Indra. "That never happens."

Connor led them through the crowd. The Warden descended the ladder, handing them a black flag with the Alpine Derby sigil stitched in silver. Connor passed it down the line. It was just cloth and thread, but it seemed like a priceless artifact.

Lining up, they performed their patrol yell again. This time, they were out of sync. Wu stomped when he should have clapped. Arlo said "grizzly bear" in place of "snowshoe hare." But it didn't matter. They had their second-place flag.

The patrol gathered next to the Wyoming Mooses. It was time to announce the winner.

Arlo realized then it was going to be Red Patrol. They had beaten the field in the initial race. They were strong at Rescue, and had no doubt done well at Teamwork. He prepared himself to clap and cheer for them when the Warden called their name.

"In first place, with ninety-three points, the winner of the forty-ninth annual Alpine Derby: Green Patrol of Pine Mountain Company."

Wu gasped. Connor looked to Indra, who quickly did the math. "They must have gotten perfect scores at every station, plus spirit." Arlo took off his gloves to applaud louder as Green Patrol made their way to the ladder to accept their first-place flag. It was larger than the others, with the sigil embroidered in gold thread.

Green Patrol's cheer was much more sophisticated, with overlapping sections performed in perfect syncopation. It had no doubt taken months to learn. When it was finished, all the Rangers cheered again.

Arlo spotted Russell Stokes clapping halfheartedly and immediately understood why Red Patrol hadn't placed in the top three.

Spirit wasn't just cheering for yourself. It was rooting for Good.

— 32 —
COURT OF HONOR

ARLO'S DAD WANTED MACARONI AND CHEESE. "Just push the phone down into it. I'll figure out a way to eat it."

Jaycee smiled. "You're disgusting." They were video-chatting with him on her phone. For a change, the meal times were reversed. It was dinner in Colorado, but breakfast in China.

"Arlo, I'm counting on you. The mac and cheese here is just awful. It's like someone saw a picture of it and didn't know what it was supposed to taste like. I'm serious. The box tastes better than what's inside."

Arlo took the phone. He held it steady while shoveling a forkful of mac and cheese into his mouth, making a big show of chewing it.

"You're torturing me. Don't you dare tell me it's delicious."

"It's so good. So cheesy."

His dad pretended to stab himself with his chopsticks.

They were eating at a long folding table in the basement of the church. It was the Ranger company's twice-yearly pot-luck dinner, a term Arlo learned meant "mostly casseroles and salad."

His mom had made baked ziti, as had four other families. Arlo tried a spoonful of each. He honestly couldn't tell them apart, even though his mom had used government cheese from the food assistance program. "Please stop calling it government cheese," she said. "It's normal cheese. They just give it to families who need a little extra help."

Between waitressing at the diner and bookkeeping for the repair shop, his mom was bringing in enough money to cover most of their expenses. But there were always surprises. One morning, they woke up to find the furnace had died and the pipes had frozen. For the next few days, Arlo had melted snow for drinking water and slept in his sleeping bag on top of his bed. It was like camping indoors.

Mitch the mechanic had helped get everything fixed. He showed Arlo where the shutoff valves were, and how to check the pipes for leaks. "It can be a small thing, just the tiniest hole. But with too much pressure, it breaks wide open." Mitch had gone to visit his daughter in New Mexico for the weekend. Arlo wondered if his mom would have invited him tonight had he been in town.

Arlo's dad asked to meet his friends, so he panned the camera over to Indra, who was sitting with the two Drs. Srinivasaraghavan-Jones. (Indra's mother was a psychologist.) Indra asked Arlo's dad about a moth that the Field Book said could only be found in Asia. "The moth is less interesting than the cocoon," she said. "You can make a tea out of it that repels scorpions."

"Why would scorpions drink tea anyway?" asked Wu.

Wu's father took the phone and began speaking Chinese with Arlo's dad. Arlo had no idea what they were saying, but there was a lot of nodding and laughing.

Meanwhile, Wu's grandfather sat sullenly at the end of the table, picking at a piece of key lime pie. Arlo asked Wu if something was wrong.

"He thought we were going to take him for a ride in the sled again. It's the only reason he came. He doesn't like big groups."

Arlo could understand. A few days earlier, he had invited Uncle Wade. Sort of. "We have the Court of Honor on Sunday night if you want to come." Wade pulled a soda from the fridge and shook his head. "That's not really my speed." Then he walked out.

Wade was spending nearly all his time in the workshop.

Arlo hadn't been inside it since the Night Mare incident. He was curious to see what his uncle was building, but didn't want to risk their tenuous friendship by pushing too hard.

Was *friendship* even the right word? Arlo had no other uncles, so he wasn't sure what was normal. But Wade felt less like a parent and more like a giant, surly kid. Arlo was convinced Wade had secrets that went beyond the contents of his workshop, but didn't know how or if he would ever uncover them.

Wu's parents handed the phone back to Jaycee. When asked about Benjy, she sighed. Arlo knew they had been fighting, but he didn't understand what had actually happened. Eavesdropping on Jaycee's side of their kitchen-phone conversations, all Arlo heard was "You're not listening to me," and "It's not what you said, it's what I heard," and "Why would you think I meant that?"

Arlo felt tremendous sympathy for Benjy.

On the other side of the table, Arlo's mom was talking with Indra's parents about boring stuff like potholes and college tuition. But then Indra's dad asked, "So, Celeste, why did you decide to move back to Pine Mountain?"

Arlo snapped to attention. He pretended to still be eating, but every brain cell was dedicated to eavesdropping on his mother's answer, filtering all other chatter.

"So, you know the situation with Clark"—Clark was

Arlo's dad—"and the government, right? I assume it's town gossip." Indra's parents nodded. "It's been a crazy couple of years. After Clark went to China, we moved around a lot, because it turns out places don't want to hire an accountant who is married to an FBI fugitive. Or rent you an apartment. Teachers tell your daughter that her father is a traitor in front of the whole class."

"I'm so sorry," said Indra's mom, touching her arm.

Arlo glanced over at Jaycee, who was happily video-chatting with their dad.

"Don't get me wrong; I'm proud of Clark," his mom continued. "He stood up for what was right. And eventually, everyone's going to see that. But it hasn't been easy." She took a sip from her paper cup of orange punch. "But you asked how we ended up in Pine Mountain. Basically, I sort of lost it one day."

Arlo tensed up with anticipation. His mom was about to answer the question he had assumed was unanswerable: What had actually happened?

"I was working a temp accounting job in Chicago," she said. "They had me in this back office with a window that looked over the parking lot. So one night, it was a Tuesday, a little after six, and the lights suddenly go out. That's odd, I think. I go up front and I realize that everyone's left. They've locked the door and set the alarm. They had forgotten I was in the back. I don't have a key. I don't have the alarm codes. I'm just a temp. I don't know who to call. Do you call the police? It's not an emergency, but it sort of is. I'm supposed to be picking up Jaycee from practice, and Arlo from after-school, and I need to make dinner, and here I am trapped in this terrible office with no way out."

"What did you do?" asked Indra's father. Arlo leaned in to listen.

"I threw a chair through the window. I climbed out, got in the car and picked up my kids. A few days later, we moved here."

Indra's mother smiled and took her hand. "Why didn't you come sooner?"

Arlo watched his mom's reaction. She seemed to be struggling to remember something, like a word on the tip of her tongue. But it never arrived. "I don't know. Pine Mountain was the last place I thought I'd end up. I can't explain why, but I had this fear of it. Like there was something buried here. But honestly, it's been amazing. I'm happier than I've been in a really long time."

Arlo wanted to lean across the table and hug his mother, but that would mean admitting he was eavesdropping. So instead he just watched as Indra's mom squeezed her hand. He wiped his eyes with his sleeve. He was pretty sure Wu spotted it.

Standing up on a chair, Christian announced it was time to start the ceremony. Everyone began clearing the tables so the patrols could put them back on the wheeled racks. Jaycee passed the phone to Arlo. "Dad wants to talk to you."

Arlo stepped over to a quiet corner. His dad moved the camera a little closer. "Hey, so. In case we cut out, I just want you to know how proud I am of you. It's great what you've been able to do there."

"Thanks."

"I promise I'm going to find a way to see you and your sister again."

"And Mom."

"And your mother. I know these last few years have been tough. But we Finches are strong. We'll get through this." Arlo nodded. "Never give up, okay? The only way you lose is when you stop trying."

———◆●◆———

After the Ranger's Vow, Arlo sat with his patrol. It was strange to be sitting down for a meeting. Usually they didn't have chairs. "It's mostly for the parents," explained Wu. "Adults just can't stand that long. They have weak bones."

Christian stepped up on the tiny stage.

"Before we get started tonight, I have an announcement. As some of you know, and many of you probably suspected, I've started working on my Bear." Indra made *told you* glances at Arlo and Wu. "I've done everything I can in Pine Mountain, so when school is out, I'll be heading off to complete my training. I want to thank all of you for letting me serve as marshal of Pine Mountain Company. It's been an honor."

Amid the murmurs, Russell Stokes shouted what everyone was thinking: "Who's taking over?"

"That's up to the council of patrol leaders." A new round of whispered conversations erupted. Everyone had an opinion.

Diana Velasquez, the Green Patrol leader, stood up and saluted. "To Christian! May his path be safe."

The Rangers responded in unison: "May his aim be true." The other Greens joined Diana in salute. Indra was the next to stand. Connor joined her, a little embarrassed. Arlo, Wu and the twins stood as well.

Senior Patrol followed shortly thereafter. Only Red Patrol stayed in their seats. Arlo could see some of them rolling their eyes. Russell pretended to throw up.

The adults and other guests started applauding, uncertain of the protocol.

Indra leaned over to whisper to Arlo and Wu. "Diana is totally going for marshal. So obvious."

"What about Tyler in Red Patrol? I know he wants it," said Wu. "Or one of the seniors?"

Indra agreed with Wu's picks. "It's going to get messy."

Arlo couldn't even conceive of the company without Christian in charge. Even though it had only been a few months, Arlo was confident no one could do the job as well. He didn't want anything to change: not here, not at home, not at school. He felt like he had just figured out how everything worked, and now the rules were being rewritten.

It was time to award badges and ranks. Each patrol went in turn, standing on the stage while the patrol leader handed out patches.

Senior Patrol went first. Two boys had earned their Trailcraeft badges, while a girl with thick glasses collected her Serpentry and Barklore. But she didn't look at all happy to receive them. "She failed her Ram trial," whispered Indra. "She'll have to try again."

Arlo was suddenly panicked, the same dread he felt when a teacher announced a surprise quiz. His own Trial of Rank had gone well, or so he thought. He had completed his Dark Walk on his first attempt, even though he'd drawn the most difficult figure (the star). He had recited the Ranger's Vow and explained what it meant. He had saluted properly and tied all the knots. He couldn't think of anything he had done wrong, and yet they'd never actually said he had passed.

Next up was Red Patrol. They mumbled and rushed through the presentation as if too cool to care. Russell Stokes collected his Wards and Arrowing badges. Kwame Wilson earned his Wolf. His mother stood up behind Arlo, taking lots of photos with her phone.

Kwame had been one of the five Rangers on Arlo's trial, but asked him no questions. Maybe because he already knew he was voting no. Arlo looked at Connor, three seats away. He was holding all of the patrol's new patches in his hand. Was one of them Arlo's Squirrel? He was certain Connor would have told him if he'd failed. That is, if he was even allowed to.

Green Patrol went next. Instead of simply reading the names and badges, Diana Velasquez had incorporated them into a rhyming poem. It was clever in places ("Watch Hope graft her Ropecraeft with Forestry for dope rafts"), but ultimately exhausting. The adults applauded much louder than the other Rangers.

Blue Patrol was last. Connor didn't attempt anything fancy as he announced Wu's badges for Watching and Pathing, and the twins' badges for Signaling and Tracking. Indra had earned all four of those as well, along with her Owl rank. As

Connor handed her the patch, Arlo could see the next one in his hand: Squirrel. "Congratulations," said Connor, shaking his hand.

The Squirrel patch was brand-new and stiff. Arlo ran his thumb over the threads that formed the squirrel and its acorn, thinking back to Uncle Wade's old patches he had taken off the shirt that first night. He looked out to the audience, where he saw his mom applauding. His sister was holding up the phone so his dad could watch.

All of the patches had been handed out, but Connor wasn't finished. "We have some special awards as well." From his cargo pockets, he pulled several stones. Arlo recognized them as the red stones Connor had used to build the wards in the Valley of Fire.

"First up, we have the award for Most Indefatigable, which is a vocab word that means 'unstoppable.' The winner is Indra Srinivasaraghavan-Jones." He handed her the rock. She smiled. They both saluted.

"Next up is Most Optimistic. This can only go to Henry Wu." The rest of the patrol cheered as Wu accepted his rock.

"For the Most In Sync Award—wow, we actually have a tie. Jonas and Julie Delgado." The twins took their stones at the same time. Then, without a word, exchanged them. Some of the parents laughed.

Connor held the final stone. "Last, we have the Special Prize for Heroism and General Bravery. No question, the award goes to Arlo Finch." Arlo accepted the rock and saluted with it in his hand. Connor saluted back.

"Patrol dismissed."

33

A VISITOR

"IT'S CUTE. I LIKE THE TAIL." Jaycee handed Arlo his Squirrel patch back. "Congratulations."

"Thanks." They were standing in front of the church, waiting for their mom, who had gone back in to retrieve the casserole dish she'd forgotten. Most of the cars had already left the parking lot.

Jaycee's phone buzzed. She checked the message. A glance to Arlo—

"It's fine," he said. "You can call Benjy."

Jaycee untangled her headphones and wandered off.

The moon was a sliver, a fingernail clipping in a sea of stars. Arlo stared at it, keenly aware of the fullness of the sphere. The shadowed section of the moon was always there, even if the light didn't fully expose it. He imagined himself standing on it, looking back at the Earth. Would he recognize the country beneath him? Or was "beneath" even the right way to think about it?

The moon was the moon. The Earth was the Earth. They were bound together, but there was no clear "above" or "below." They were simply sideways to each other, forever spinning through the darkness.

"Quite a moon tonight." A man was standing beside him. Arlo hadn't heard him approach. He was small for a grownup, with a mustache that twisted up into points. He was wearing a wool jacket, leather boots and a fur hat. "That's a hunter's moon if I ever saw one."

Arlo didn't recognize him, but he didn't know most of the Rangers' parents. "Actually, a hunter's moon is full." Every Ranger knew that. It was in the Field Book.

"Try hunting during a full moon and you'll go hungry. Your dinner will see you coming." He had a trace of an accent. Arlo couldn't place it, but it sounded old-timey. "Congratulations, incidentally. Quite a thing you did."

Arlo had forgotten he was holding the patch. "Almost everyone gets Squirrel."

"Not that. The bit in the Woods. That was unique." The man looked over. His eyes were pale, almost silver. It wasn't just the moonlight.

"You're one of them, aren't you?" asked Arlo. The man smiled. His teeth were perfectly white. And sharp. "You're one of the people beyond the Woods."

The man shook his head. "I'm not people. I just dress up sometimes."

"What are you?"

"You can call me Fox." There was no "mister" in front of his name—if it even was a name. Arlo suspected it might be his true form.

"What do you want?"

"To meet the hero! Quite a thing, defeating a hag. That very one nearly took my tail when I was a pup."

Arlo turned to face him directly. "Why was she trying to kill me?"

"For the bounty." He rubbed his fingers together. "There's a price on your head, Arlo Finch. At least there was. Now some are thinking you may be worth more alive than dead."

"Why? What do they want?"

"Something hidden. Something you may be able to find. But that's for another season. I'll come back when it's warmer." He adjusted the collar of his coat, preparing to leave.

Arlo grabbed the man's arm. "Am I still in danger?"

Fox laughed. "A squirrel is always in danger." He lifted Arlo's hand off his sleeve. "But keep your spirits up, Mr. Finch. This is where it gets most exciting."

The man took a step forward, pushing past him. With a gust of wind, he was gone. Arlo turned to see his mother approaching. She was carrying the casserole dish.

"You ready?" she asked.

Arlo nodded. He was.

This book is dedicated to scouts and explorers—both the ones I grew up with and the ones who inspire me every day.

—J.A.

DON'T MISS

* * *

ARLO FINCH
IN THE LAKE OF THE MOON

* * *

COMING SPRING 2019

THE ADVENTURE CONTINUES...

SCHOOL'S OUT, AND SUMMER HAS BEGUN. Arlo and the Rangers of Pine Mountain Company are headed to Camp Redfeather for two weeks of archery, canoeing and investigating the ancient monster who lurks in the lake's icy waters.

But before they've even gotten on the bus, a major discovery puts Arlo, Indra and Wu in new jeopardy. Forces from beyond the Long Woods are after a mysterious item that only Arlo can recover. Meanwhile, the normally gentle forest spirits seem aligned against him.

New faces and sudden departures change the dynamics of the Blue Patrol. But it's the mystery of the long-lost Yellow Patrol that sends Arlo across the Lake of the Moon and into a thrilling new adventure. Once he uncovers the secret history Uncle Wade has been protecting, nothing will ever be the same.

DISCUSSION QUESTIONS

The Ranger's Vow begins with the words "Loyal, brave, kind and true."

1. What does it mean to be **loyal**? Arlo describes loyalty as "a promise you never needed to make." Is Arlo always loyal to his friends and family?

2. In what ways is Arlo **brave**? Does *brave* mean the same thing as *unafraid*? What does Arlo's mom teach him about bravery?

3. Is being **kind** the same as not being cruel? What are examples of kindness in *Valley of Fire*? What examples can you think of from your own life?

4. What second meaning of **true** does Arlo learn from Christian? Are loyalty and truth related?

5. If you were writing the Ranger's Vow, what other qualities would you add to this list?

In *Valley of Fire*, Arlo learns about the Wonder, the mysterious force that helps keep the magic of the Long Woods a secret.

6. What have you encountered in your life that you couldn't capture in a photograph?

7. The adults in Pine Mountain seem to be unaware of the magic in their own backyards. In what ways do you think kids and grown-ups see things differently?

8. If you could learn one of the skills demonstrated in *Valley of Fire*—such as snaplights, thunderclaps or slipknaughts—which would you choose, and why?

Like many books, *Valley of Fire* is told from a third-person limited perspective. This means that as readers, we know only what Arlo knows, and can "look inside" only his mind.

9. How would the story be different if it were told from the point of view of Indra, or Wu? What would it be like from Jaycee's perspective?

10. Uncle Wade seems to know more than he's telling, particularly about the Yellow Patrol. What do you think the secret might be?